P9-CLL-476

"You believe me," Victoria said with relief.

"I believe something is going on," Jeff corrected. "I just don't really understand what yet."

She grabbed the stair railing and followed after him. "Where will we go? Your car is destroyed—"

Jeff frowned but didn't slow down. Surely an idea would come to him by the first floor. He pushed his legs to go faster. Adrenaline always helped clear his mind.

He was so focused on the anger from his car being blown up that he wasn't being considerate of Victoria. "I know where we're going. Follow me." Once they reached the bottom stair, he turned to her. "You sure you're okay?"

"I'm not going to let anything slow me down with that creep trying to find us. Where to?"

His hands hovered over the exit sign on the door. "Stay close to me, okay?"

Victoria tapped his shoulder. "Jeff. Security cameras."

"Then let's hope our security breach friend isn't watching right now."

HEATHER WOODHAVEN

earned her pilot's license, rode a hot air balloon over the safari lands of Kenya, assisted an engineer with a medical laser in a Haitian mission, went parasailing over Caribbean seas, lived through an accidental detour onto a black diamond ski trail in the Aspens and snorkeled among stingrays before becoming a mother of three and wife of one (her greatest adventure). She's filled many jobs such as travel agent, business executive, children's minister, aerobic instructor and preschool teacher. Heather channels her love for adventure into writing characters who find themselves in extraordinary circumstances.

CALCULATED RISK

HEATHER WOODHAVEN

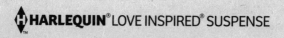

If you purchased this book without a cover you should be aware that this book is stolen property. It was reported as "unsold and destroyed" to the publisher, and neither the author nor the publisher has received any payment for this "stripped book."

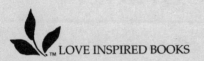

LOVE INSPIRED BOOKS

Recycling programs
for this product may
not exist in your area.

ISBN-13: 978-0-373-44647-6

Calculated Risk

Copyright © 2015 by Heather Humrichouse

All rights reserved. Except for use in any review, the reproduction or utilization of this work in whole or in part in any form by any electronic, mechanical or other means, now known or hereinafter invented, including xerography, photocopying and recording, or in any information storage or retrieval system, is forbidden without the written permission of the editorial office, Love Inspired Books, 233 Broadway, New York, NY 10279 U.S.A.

This is a work of fiction. Names, characters, places and incidents are either the product of the author's imagination or are used fictitiously, and any resemblance to actual persons, living or dead, business establishments, events or locales is entirely coincidental.

This edition published by arrangement with Love Inspired Books.

® and TM are trademarks of Love Inspired Books, used under license. Trademarks indicated with ® are registered in the United States Patent and Trademark Office, the Canadian Intellectual Property Office and in other countries.

www.Harlequin.com

Printed in U.S.A.

For God hath not given us the spirit of fear;
but of power, and of love, and of a sound mind.
—*2 Timothy* 1:7

For my parents who developed my love of adventure and storytelling. For my husband who refused to let me give up on my dream and continues to read everything I write. For my children who cheer me on. And to the many other friends and family members who continue to encourage me.

Thank you.

ONE

Victoria Hayes tossed through her anxious dreams, the day's events on an endless loop: Todd Wagner had caught her trying to collect evidence. Wagner's breath was hot and pungent against her neck, just like her dog's breath. And he was barking.

Barking?

Victoria blinked herself awake with the help of Baloo's wet nose pressed into her cheek. The acrid smell of smoke and the piercing shriek of the house's smoke alarms sent her heart into overdrive. She couldn't see anything. The haze stung her eyes. The urge to yell for help prompted her to open her mouth, but her lungs constricted and sent her into a fit of coughing.

She kicked against the covers and fell off the bed, landing on the plush carpet. The fur of her one-hundred-fifty-pound Newfoundland brushed against her hand. She reached out and felt for his tail. Victoria crawled a few steps. It was useless. She couldn't see a thing. She reached out again and felt for his presence. Baloo, like his fellow Newfoundlands, was acting like the rescue dog he'd been bred to be as he led her to safety. Victoria never knew he had it in him.

Her hands crossed the hallway threshold. If she and Baloo could reach the entryway, they had a fighting chance. Wiping tears away with the back of her hand, she could make out hot orange flames licking the ceiling ahead of them.

Victoria cowered to the floor and pressed her face against the carpet as another fit of coughing shook her. Every muscle in her body wanted to give up, wanted to sleep. Baloo ran around and nudged her.

One hand, one knee, one move at a time, she obeyed Baloo's nudges with her eyes closed. She couldn't see anyway. Her skin burned from the heat. She prayed for help just as Baloo shoved her again. An unbidden image of the grass, a river and an open starlit sky filled her mind, and she forced herself to move faster.

Her head bumped into glass. *Thank you, Lord.* She reached up and pulled on the sliding door handle. Flicking the back door lock upward, she wrenched it open and sucked in a breath of fresh air.

She heard it before she felt it—the roar—as the fire sucked up the new current of oxygen. In the light of the new flames, Victoria glimpsed a sight of the shiny red bag just out of reach, on the kitchen counter. Against her better judgment, Victoria took a step into the kitchen and grabbed the purse. Baloo barked, bit the bottom of her pajama pant leg and dragged her the rest of the way outside.

Victoria stumbled across the cement patio, following Baloo, who trotted across the yard to the gate. She reached into her purse, and as soon as her fingers found her phone she heard distant sirens already on the way. Her voice probably wasn't strong enough to communicate, anyway. Her feet moved quickly over the icy wet grass to her waiting rescuer. She flung the gate open and prayed Baloo wouldn't run off, as he was prone to do without a leash.

Victoria wiped her gritty eyes with the corner of her pajama shirt. Baloo led her to the wooded nature trail that ran past the backyards of their subdivision. Beyond the grove of trees, the Boise River flowed. Ironic. If only she had means to redirect all that water or a rainstorm were to sweep over the neighborhood.

Her breath caught as she watched the flames climb the siding of her house. *Please, don't let the fire hit the other homes or these woods, Lord.* She fell to her knees in a pile of leaves and hugged Baloo as she coughed the toxic fumes out of her system.

"Thank you. You saved me," she whispered to her beloved canine.

Baloo made a gagging noise. She released him so he could clear the smoke from his own lungs. Victoria leaned back on her heels and watched her home continue to be consumed by fire. Her cheeks were wet with tears as she recalled the many hours she'd spent picking out paint colors, wall accents and furniture. The painstaking process of making her house a home seemed futile—all that effort to open her doors to neighbors, friends, book clubs and Bible studies. And for what? It was all going up in smoke.

Victoria's gut churned. She hadn't lit any candles. She hadn't cooked her own dinner. She even turned her computer off before bed.

Her computer…Victoria groaned. The flash drive containing the evidence sat inside the house, likely a melted piece of useless plastic by now. Her only hope of proving her suspicions gone, and now she had nothing to take to the FBI in the morning.

Could that be why her home was destroyed, because Wagner caught her trying to gather evidence of fraud? Was she in danger?

Baloo's cough morphed into a growl. Victoria fell back in alarm. The moonlight illuminated Baloo's position, four feet away. The fur on the back of his neck spiked, and his nose pointed to the grove of trees behind her. She twisted around and stared into the blackness between the trees.

"What is it, boy?" His focus and steadfast growl made her shiver.

Victoria leaped to her feet. She clutched her phone as she stepped backward, back onto the nature path. Her feet protested as a sharp rock pressed into her arch. A sudden snap of a twig, and Baloo's monstrous bark pushed her into gear.

"Come! Baloo!" She patted hard against her leg as she ran. Baloo obeyed, as Victoria sprinted toward the far side of her neighbor's house—one she knew had no fence. Darting between the two houses, she lengthened her stride to reach the street in record time.

She spotted her car parked a couple houses down on the street, almost directly in front of the raging bonfire. A block farther down sat a red Range Rover. The same vehicle she suspected followed her yesterday afternoon.

The disoriented feeling vanished immediately. Pieces clicked into place within her mind. It was no coincidence that Baloo growled at the trees. She glanced over her shoulder. A figure in the shadows crept into the front yard behind her, two houses down, and he was headed her way.

"Don't make me shoot you," she shouted in his direction. The only weapon in her possession was the pepper spray in her purse, but the figure in the shadows didn't need to know that. He momentarily stiffened. If only she could see the man's face, but she didn't want to risk standing out in the open any longer. What if he had a gun?

Her hand fumbled within her purse for her keys. Where was that fire truck? She needed help.

"Victoria!"

She spun to find her neighbor beckoning to her from the porch across the street. With a quick look over her shoulder, Victoria raced to Darcy's house. Lunging into Darcy's outstretched arms, Victoria fell to her knees one step within her foyer, coughing.

A blurry vision of Darcy waving at someone swam before her eyes. A man wearing a helmet pushed Baloo away from her side and shoved a mask onto her face. The sweet oxygen eased the pain in her lungs. She let herself close her eyes, but she needed to hang on to her thoughts. She didn't have time to lose consciousness.

Tonight was no accidental house fire, and she needed real help. Everything she'd worked for was at risk. She couldn't start over. Not again. And there was only one person she could think of who might be able to help her.

Jeff Tucker.

Jeff Tucker squinted at his alarm clock. Who would be ringing his doorbell at four in the morning? He grabbed his cell phone on the way to the door.

He flipped on the porch light and peeked through the peephole. His lead accountant at Earth Generators, Inc. recoiled in the bright light. She closed her eyes and waved at the door. *What in the world?*

Jeff did a quick assessment of his own appearance. He

supposed his blue flannel pajama pants and navy T-shirt were modest enough to answer the door in the middle of the night. He unlocked the bolt and swung the door open only to see a large beast just to Victoria's right. The dog knocked him to the side and trotted indoors. "Hey!"

Victoria held a hand to her mouth. "I am so sorry, Jeff. He's kind of my protector right now. He usually has better manners."

Jeff squinted. "Victoria, what's going on? And why does your dog smell like a barbecue?"

She responded by glancing over her left shoulder and then her right. "I think I'm in danger. Can I explain inside? Please?"

Jeff's mouth dropped open, but he moved back and opened the door wider. "Yes, of course." She stepped in and immediately to the left of the door, flat against the wall, as if she didn't want anyone to see her. He closed the door. "Want me to call the police?"

"Someone set my house on fire tonight. The police already know but have nothing to go on yet."

Jeff raked his hand through his hair. So many questions came to mind. He started with the most obvious. "Your house was on fire?" Jeff blinked. "Are you okay?" He examined her once more. Her face appeared paler than normal, and her bright blue eyes were red from crying…or smoke? His first aid training kicked in gear. Victoria could be in shock, which would explain her bizarre decision to come to his house. "I can drive you to the hospital now."

"No, I'm fine. The paramedics checked me out." She crossed her arms, and her teeth chattered. "Sorry. I just can't seem to get warm."

Jeff turned to the basket by his couch. "I think I have a blanket here somewhere."

She eagerly accepted the red fleece and swung it around herself like a robe. She flipped her long hair out from under the blanket. It looked wet; no wonder she couldn't get warm.

"My neighbor let me borrow her clothes and take a shower, but I didn't think of a jacket. Everything of mine is—" her voice caught "—gone."

"That's horrible. How can I help?"

Victoria's face crumpled. "I'm sorry to barge in on you in the middle of the night. I had to talk to you, and I remembered where you lived from the department Christmas party."

She shifted her gaze to the ceiling, then the living room walls. She looked everywhere, it seemed, but at him. "Jeff, I need you to come with me to work. It can't wait."

Jeff's arms fell to his side. Did she realize most people considered four in the morning to be the middle of the night? "I better start a cup of coffee while you explain."

"No. There's no time. I need you to go with me to the office. Now."

Jeff turned toward the sudden slamming noise in the living room. The mammoth dog flopped down on the rug at his back door. The baseball bat-sized tail pounded a couple more times on the glass. "Make yourself at home," he muttered. How was it possible that Victoria—beautiful, sweet, off-limits Victoria—could be in his home, like this? And why did she need him? He wasn't an accountant or a police officer; he was a supervisor.

"I think you're the only one that can help me," she said, as if hearing his thoughts.

"How do you figure?"

She took a deep breath and swung her black, velvet hair over her shoulder. "Can I explain it in the car? Please?"

The image of her, wrapped in his blanket in his living room, suddenly felt too intimate. Going to the office—or anywhere else—seemed like a good idea. "Give me five minutes." Jeff closed his bedroom door behind him and flipped on the light. He slapped his face a couple times while watching his reflection in the mirror. He definitely wasn't dreaming. Confusion and annoyance were evident from his expression, but it was the best he could do at this hour. He threw on jeans and a shirt.

The dog growled from the other room.

"Jeff!"

He shoved his feet into already tied shoes and ran out of his room. The dog's large mouth lifted up and over its teeth, in preparation to bite something...or someone.

Victoria whipped around to face him. "There was a man lurking down there in your backyard." She pointed at the back glass door.

Jeff's shoulders relaxed. "Well, it's more of a community area." The moment he said the words, he knew it was a weak attempt at comforting her. The dog turned around in a circle a couple of times and plopped back down on to the rug.

She blew out a long breath. "He must be gone, or Baloo wouldn't relax. I'm sure of it," Victoria said, but it seemed as if she was talking more to herself than to him. She turned her attention to Jeff. "Ready to go?"

Her concern about a lurking man may have diminished, but his only increased. "If you're right and think someone is after you, I don't know how safe it is to walk to your car in the open. Even with me and the gorilla by your side."

A flash of anger sparked in her eyes, and Jeff was reminded how badly he needed coffee. He wasn't guarding his tongue very well without it.

"He's a Newfoundland. And a great rescuer."

He smiled at the dog in hopes of appeasing Victoria. "I'm sorry." The possibility of a man waiting in the shadows changed things. Jeff wasn't armed or trained in defensive techniques. "What are we dealing with?"

She raised an eyebrow and pursed her lips. He'd never seen her look annoyed before. At work, she was nothing but quiet and efficient. She faced the window again. "Last quarter I reviewed the expense reports before submitting them to the audit committee."

He nodded. "Like every quarter."

"Yes, but when the numbers went public, they seemed different than I remembered."

Jeff shifted his feet. Maybe he should've taken a seat first. "What do you mean?"

"The numbers made Earth Generators, Inc. look like a much better company than reality. The profits are way up and the expenses are way down. The difference in operating and capital expenses grew exponentially."

"Okay. Hang on a second." Jeff pressed his thumbs into his temples, attempting to fight off the headache threatening to start. "So, in English, that means the stockholders are about to be very rich."

She tilted her head to the left and right, as if weighing his translation. "Essentially, yes. Except, the numbers were blatantly wrong, Jeff. I'm sure of it."

Victoria consistently proved to be the best accountant in his department. It's why she'd risen to lead accountant within a year. Normally, he'd believe her in a heartbeat, but she was standing in his living room with her massive dog at four in the morning. Had she lost her mind?

"The problem was—when I checked the data again—everything matched the public numbers."

"So you misremembered."

She blinked and shook her head. "No, I don't think I did. But your reaction proves my point. I knew I needed evidence."

Jeff winced but covered it by taking long strides into the kitchen. She may think they had no time to waste, but if he didn't at least get some instant coffee into his system, he wouldn't be able to retain a single word she said.

Victoria followed him to the sink. "So, this time around, at the end of the quarter, I took action. I saved my own copy of the report onto a flash drive before submitting it to Wagner and the audit committee. Then, when the report became public yesterday, I went into work early—before everyone else—to see if the numbers matched the statements on my flash drive."

"And?"

She folded her arms across her chest. "I was right on the money, Jeff. Someone changed the numbers in the company files and the public reports." She took a deep breath and rubbed her hands over her arms. "Except Wagner caught me comparing the reports."

Jeff's spoonful of coffee grounds froze in midair. While Jeff was supervisor of the accounts payable department, Todd Wagner managed the entire accounting division. In fact, Wagner had just reassigned Jeff to supervisor of the accounts receivable department starting next week.

Jeff frowned. "Victoria, listen. I've always respected

your opinion and your work ethic. But Wagner is my boss, too, so I'm not sure this is the best way to communicate any prob—"

"Please." She bit her lip and made eye contact for a brief second. "Please, hear me out. Wagner implied that I better be careful…that someone might suspect me of insider trading. Even though I didn't do anything wrong."

Jeff rubbed the spot between his eyebrows. "I think I'm missing something."

"Wagner ordered me to meet him after work for drinks. He said I would regret it if I didn't show up."

A chill ran up his spine. He clenched his jaw and mixed the spoonful of instant coffee into a mug of tap water. If Wagner was harassing Victoria…Jeff took a deep breath to remain professional. "This sounds like a matter for Human Resources. I know April in HR well enough that I can arrange an emergency meeting first thing tomorrow—I mean today."

She smirked. "I know April, too, but that won't help. I slipped out of work an hour early to avoid Wagner. Then, a red Range Rover started following me everywhere I went. The grocery store, the dry cleaners, the gym…it even pulled up next to me. This guy in a ball cap made frantic gestures at me, like my car had a flat tire. He motioned for me to pull over, but instead I drove straight to the auto shop." She took a shaky breath. "Jeff, there was nothing wrong with my tires. It was a lie to try to get me to pull over."

Jeff stared at her for a moment, imagining what could've happened had she pulled over. Victoria stared at his hands. He followed her gaze to find them in fists and purposefully relaxed them. "I'm glad you thought fast, but, Victoria, even you have to admit there are a lot of Range Rovers in town."

Her blue eyes narrowed. "I know what I saw. The same red car was on my street when the fire started, and gone by the time the police arrived." She tightened the blanket around her shoulders. "I think Wagner is the reason I'm in danger. If I'm right, he's making millions while committing fraud. If he gets away with it, the stockholders and employees will be the ones to suffer. I need your help to prove it. I don't dare go into work alone again."

Jeff gulped down the disgusting, lukewarm instant coffee. He tried out the idea of his boss as an embezzler, a mastermind of fraud. Was it possible? Wagner wasn't someone who valued people skills. He lived in a fancy house and liked to show off his latest purchases. He also seemed to be a man who prided himself on a job well done. Jeff placed the mug in the sink. "Why not go to the police? Or even the FBI?"

"How can the police help me when I have nothing solid to give them? I made an appointment with the FBI yesterday, for this morning. But now—" Her gaze dropped to her intertwined hands. She sighed. "I have nothing to give them."

"I thought you had the evidence on a flash drive."

She turned her attention to his wall clock. "It burned to a crisp in the fire." She looked back at him. "So, do you understand the urgency? We need to go now, Jeff. Before they see where I hid a copy of the file. I'm…I'm a little worried they won't stop until I'm dead."

Her phone vibrated and simultaneously released a loud alarm. She looked down at it. "Someone is breaking into my car!"

TWO

Victoria ran back into the living room. "I need to get to a window!" She passed the couch and slid two wooden blinds apart to see through the window closest to her car.

"What's going on?"

"My brother put a car alarm application on my phone. He said it's more effective than an alarm on your car because it alerts you, not the crook." Victoria squinted out the window. A man wearing a baseball cap had one knee on the passenger seat, rifling through her glove box.

"I think my brother was right." The man looked up. Victoria jerked away from the window and gasped. "What if he saw me?" She put a hand on her chest. "I parked in the guest parking lot just in case I was being followed. I had hoped he wouldn't know which town house I was visiting."

"I'm calling the police." Jeff grabbed his phone off the end table and took her place at the window.

Victoria nodded mutely. Her throat burned with the threat of tears. Her house was a pile of used matchsticks, and she was acting like a crazy woman begging Jeff for help. She caught sight of a small navy leather book on the end table by the couch. A Bible. The confirmation that she'd come to the right man steadied her pulse.

Jeff gave ethics lessons on taking pens from work to use for personal reasons. He also knew only the bare minimum about accounting, but that wasn't his job. He was there to manage employees, and the job suited him. He was considered the most eligible bachelor at work, so much so that April—one of her friends at work—had staked her claim. The last time she'd stopped by Victoria's cubicle to say hi, April had said she was dating Jeff.

Victoria cringed. Would April be upset that she'd gone to Jeff for help? She hadn't even told any of her friends about her suspicions, fearing that she was wrong. If only April had access to the accounting divisions, then Victoria could've gone to her for help instead.

Jeff's strong voice filtered through her thoughts. "There's a suspicious man just inside the entrance of Greenbelt Townhomes. He's opening and rifling through my friend's car." He rattled off his address and thanked them.

Baloo's head slid underneath her hand. He always seemed to sense her emotions and track her down when she most needed comfort. Victoria patted his head in appreciation. Baloo's giant tail smacked the wooden lamp off the end table just as Jeff hung up.

Victoria picked up the lamp, thankful it was still in one piece, and gave Jeff a sheepish grin. "If you could help me grab that evidence, I'll give my story to the FBI, and be out of your hair."

Jeff stared at the dog. "That simple, huh?" He held up the phone. "They're on their way. If you're right—if Wagner's involved—we need to get to the office now.

He's usually there by 6:00 a.m. Since your car is being ransacked at the moment, let's take mine."

Victoria warred between embarrassment and anger at his reaction. Hadn't she been trying to hurry him to the office? She followed Jeff downstairs, past a small room that held no furniture. Snowshoes, skis, fishing equipment and camping gear lined the walls. Baloo seemed to sense her anxiety as he trotted behind her.

Jeff frowned. "I'm sorry. There are only two seats."

Her mouth dropped open at the sight of his car. He drove a two-seater silver Honda S2000 convertible—a beautiful sports car but without any room for a massive dog. "I'm afraid Nana will have to stay here."

"Baloo," she corrected. Her dog sniffed, as if indignant. "And it's a he," she added.

"Sorry. He looks like the dog from Peter Pan."

She nodded. "He's the same breed as Nana."

He grinned. "You must like Disney movies." He leaned down and patted Baloo's head. "As long as you trust him here, I'm sure he'll be fine."

Victoria looked back hesitantly. Her dog's concerned face mimicked her own. Baloo's ears pressed backward, and he lifted his nose up in the air. She stared back into the dog's eyes, racking her brain for another solution. She really didn't have a choice, though.

Without waiting for her answer, Jeff walked back to the basement with Victoria and Baloo following and picked up a bowl from the camping dinnerware. He walked through another door to his right and emerged with a clean bowl of water. She stood, frozen in place, as she watched him care for Baloo. The kindness may have been directed at the dog, but the gesture took her off guard. "You have no idea how much I appreciate this."

He glanced her way and nodded. She'd only seen him dress casually once before—at the department Christmas party he'd hosted at his place. And now, wearing dark jeans, a checkered navy-and-brown flannel button-down shirt and brown hiking shoes, he looked more like Baloo's owner than she did. She caught sight of his mountain bike leaning up against the wall. He must be a true outdoorsman. No wonder all the ladies at work flirted openly with him.

But not Victoria.

She'd never fall for a man like that, no matter how nice a guy he might be. She'd been burned before. And now she knew how to weigh men like numbers. She could identify a risk or a safe investment within minutes of conversing. She didn't need conversation to peg Jeff. A ruggedly handsome and charming man was high risk, pure and simple. Beg for his help, though? Well, that was an entirely different matter.

After she buckled her seat belt a few moments later, Jeff turned off the lights to the garage, kept the car's headlights off and slowly backed out of the town house driveway and onto the street.

"Shouldn't the police be here by now?" Victoria whispered.

Jeff shrugged. "I certainly would've thought so." He pressed the brakes. "I'm tempted to drive over there."

"Please, don't." Her hand jutted out and touched his shoulder. "I don't want him to see us together. I can't stand the thought of him targeting you because of me. He torched my house. For all we know, he might be armed and start targeting you. Let's hurry. This is our chance while he's busy."

Jeff considered her for the briefest of moments and

then glanced down at her hand, still on his shoulder. She jerked her hand back and stared out the window. If only she could crawl underneath the seat and hide. Less than an hour alone together and she was already sending him the wrong message. She had meant what she'd said, but there was no need to put her hand on his shoulder...his very strong shoulder.

Jeff swung the car in the opposite direction, and a minute later, flipped on his headlights. "So, how do we gather evidence if someone's already changed the reports?"

Victoria rifled through her purse and pulled out her security badge. "I saved a separate copy on the office server underneath a miscellaneous receipts file. I'm hoping no one's found it yet."

They rode in silence the short distance to the office. Jeff parked the car at the far end of the company lot. "Do you want to wait here and send me in for it?"

Victoria examined herself. Her neighbor's clothes were not only big on her, but also outdated in style, and not very flattering. She wore a pink cardigan with pearl buttons, brown dress pants and black loafers. "I'd be lying if I said no, but I also think it'd be more efficient if we just get it done together. Do you have a flash drive we can use in your office?"

"No, but I can email it somewhere."

Victoria shook her head. "You can't email a file like that. It'll get filtered. Anything over twenty-five megabytes gets blocked." She flicked her hand in the air. "Believe me, I already tried."

"Then I'll burn it onto a disk. I'm hoping to get you somewhere safe and still have time to go back home and change before the official workday starts." He leaned over and pulled his office badge out of the glove compartment.

She pressed herself back into the leather seat at his sudden close proximity. He even smelled good. She inhaled deeply and caught a whiff of pine trees and cedar.

Victoria bit her lip. If she couldn't find the evidence, then this would effectively prove to Jeff that she was a crazy flake. She'd been there, done that. She couldn't afford to lose her reputation and, most likely, her job. How would she ever get hired again? This was her last chance.

Victoria slung her purse over her shoulder and walked to the office entrance, her head held high. They stepped inside the glass lobby and strode to the automatic sliding glass door.

A security guard at the oval station gave Jeff a nod. Jeff touched her shoulder. "Go on up. I know this guard. He might have seen the Range Rover yesterday. I'll catch up in a minute."

Victoria wanted to object but followed his gaze. She recognized the guard but doubted he remembered her. She gave a thumbs-up and held up her badge to the keypad that opened the elevators. It made a high-pitched sound, followed by an off-pitch buzz. Her face heated, and she could feel the guard's eye on her. "That's weird," she said nonchalantly. She held up her badge again, only to produce the same horrible sound.

"Maybe we're not allowed until our shift?" Victoria asked, realizing how silly her question sounded.

Jeff shook his head. "No. I've been here before on a Saturday to catch up on work after I had the flu. I've never had a problem before."

The security guard left his station and walked up to them. "What seems to be the problem?"

Victoria hoped Jeff could see the panic in her eyes. He responded by smiling at the guard. "Hey, Charlie. Victoria's badge isn't working. Can she use her driver's license instead?"

Charlie frowned. "As much as I'd like to do that, I can't. There's quite the process if your badge doesn't work. Did you bend it, snap it?"

"No, nothing like that," she replied. Her heart raced. Had Wagner already fired her? He had told her she'd regret not meeting him after work.

Charlie looked between the two of them. "I'll see what I can do, but I might need to call a higher-up." He waved them over to his station and opened his hand. Victoria handed over the badge, and he slid it underneath a stationary scanner.

The high-pitched buzz echoed around the glass walls. "Well, that's strange." He peered over his glasses at her. "Says here that your account doesn't exist."

"What?" Jeff leaned over the counter. "That's got to be a mistake. She was working here just yesterday. I'm her supervisor in the…"

"Oh, I haven't forgotten who you are, Jeff," the guard interrupted, fingering Victoria's badge. "And I haven't forgotten Victoria here either. She's the one that's always leaving homemade fudge for me and the guys in the break room." He flashed a smile. "You didn't think we were going let the chef of those goodies remain a secret, now did you? Got too many retired police detectives in our department for that."

Victoria's cheeks heated. Not so much from the guard's good-natured ribbing but more from Jeff's surprised stare. Apparently, she wasn't that adept at doing a good deed in secret, no matter how hard she tried. Victoria shrugged. "It's nothing, really. I like to cook. I just don't want the temptation to eat it all."

Charlie held up his closed fingers to his mouth. "She makes peanut butter fudge so smooth, it melts on your tongue. Even wraps it up in fancy homemade boxes that the wife loves to keep." Charlie sighed. "But, I'm afraid without a call to my supervisor, I can't help you." He lifted up the phone to his ear. "It'll be a few moments, folks."

Victoria held her hand out toward Charlie's arm. "Would you mind if we just waited until normal business hours? I can stay here while Jeff checks on a very important report for me."

Charlie looked between the two of them and hung up the phone. "I can do one better. There's no rule against Jeff signing you in as a guest."

"Oh, that would be great. Then we can go home and change and deal with this whole mess when I get back. Right, Jeff?"

"Well," Charlie mused, "this isn't my normal shift, but I'm sure I can leave a note for the next guy."

Victoria smiled sweetly. "It's okay. I don't mind going through it all again. No sense in making any more paperwork for you."

Charlie's eyebrow rose, but he said nothing. Instead, he handed a clipboard to Jeff. "Just sign her in there."

Jeff complied. "Hey, Charlie, there's been some guy in a red Range Rover bothering Victoria after work. If you could just keep an eye out for him in the future, that'd be great."

"Is that so? We'll keep a watch out for him, Miss Hayes." Charlie raised a hand in acknowledgment.

When Jeff swiped his badge, the elevator doors

opened swiftly, and they stepped inside. Victoria worried her hands. "Thank you for asking him to keep a look out. I'm wondering if we shouldn't have come here." She turned to him. "I'm sorry I dragged you into this, really. I couldn't see another option."

"My curiosity is definitely piqued now. A few too many things are happening for this to all be a coincidence."

She inhaled sharply. "My house went up in flames tonight. You saw a man rifling through my car. You still thought they were coincidences?"

Jeff held up both hands in surrender. "I'm not saying I didn't believe you, I just hoped you were wrong." He crossed his arms over his chest. "I don't like what the alternative means."

While it still irked her that he hadn't instantly accepted the truth based on her word, her shoulders relaxed. The elevator opened to a darkened fourth floor. Goose bumps on her arms insisted she was entering a danger zone. The motion-activated fluorescents welcomed them by flickering in a domino effect down one cubicle row. Without windows in the department, the rest of the open room remained eerily dark.

THREE

Jeff strode toward his office. Was it a coincidence that Wagner was moving him out of this department at the end of the day? He hadn't told Victoria yet; no one else knew, in fact, but Wagner and Human Resources. There would be an announcement around lunch today. Victoria had come to him because he was her supervisor. If he told her now that she'd have a new supervisor come Monday, he couldn't predict what her reaction would be, given the circumstances. So, for her sake, it was probably best to wait.

In fact, Victoria was full of surprises. She'd always been polite and answered his friendly attempts at conversation, but never beyond the bare minimum. She never initiated the conversation, either, unless it was work related. It seemed like she was friendly with everyone else in the department, and yet, she made goodies for only the security department. Why had she never brought her famous fudge to their break room? Perhaps he'd mistaken her aloofness for being shy?

He slowed his steps. Victoria wasn't following. He turned to find her frozen, white as a sheet, barely outside of the elevator.

"We're just here collecting a report. We're not trying to expose fraud, jeopardize thousands of people's financial portfolios, risk our jobs and ultimately shut the entire company down." Victoria said the words rapid-fire and stared ahead, but it was as if she wasn't seeing anything at all.

Was the shock from the fire catching up with her? He reached out for her hand. "You're freezing." He placed his other hand on top of her wrist in an attempt to warm her. "Hey. We're just trying to get the truth. Nothing more."

He leaned down a bit so she couldn't avoid eye contact. "Victoria, you're here because you're a good employee. You care about doing the right thing."

That seemed to do it. She blinked and looked straight into his eyes for the first time he could remember. He sucked in a breath at the intensity of her stare and his own sudden attraction. She glanced down at his hands over hers. The color in her cheeks made her blue eyes contrast with her dark hair. She was beautiful. Realizing his gesture came across as intimate, he dropped her wrist like a hot potato and straightened. "We don't have much time before Wagner will arrive. Let's find the files and get you to that FBI appointment. I'll sort out what the deal is with your security clearance later."

"Thank you," she said softly. Victoria stood behind him when he took a seat at his desk. "Just so you know, I don't usually freak out like that, but I've also never had someone try to kill me before either."

"Well, that would do it," Jeff mumbled, logging into the mainframe. He needed to focus on the task ahead and get her off his mind. "Now where'd you hide the file?"

She tried to direct him through the catalog of records, but she kept sighing and pointing at the screen over and over. Clearly, she was getting frustrated with his less-than-speedy computer skills. He wasn't an accountant or a computer specialist; he was a supervisor who put in the time to work his way up the ladder.

She confirmed his suspicions when she pointed to his mouse. "May I?"

"Sure," he said, and dropped his hands. Jeff intended to scoot back and let her have the chair, but she caught him off guard by leaning over his shoulder and reaching for the mouse. Her long hair swung down as a curtain between her face and his. Instead of focusing on the screen, he let his eyes close for the briefest of seconds as the coconut aroma enveloped him.

"It's still there!"

Her exclamation snapped him from his thoughts. Victoria took a step back. He could see the file on the monitor, but the bald security guard standing in his doorway didn't give him the chance to examine any further.

"I'm afraid I need to ask you to step away from the computer. We have a security breach. I need to escort you and your guest out of the building. We're asking everyone to go home until the all clear is given."

Victoria stiffened beside him. "A security breach?"

"Yes, ma'am. Please step away from the computer."

Jeff put a hand on Victoria's back. "After you." He looked directly at the guard, trying to recall if he'd ever seen him, but the man's beady eyes darted around the room. "Is this really necessary? Charlie could've just called me."

The man stared straight ahead. "Charlie is out, investigating."

Jeff leaned forward. "The security breach?"

The man nodded but didn't meet Jeff's gaze. Why did

he feel as if this man was hiding something? Jeff stepped toward the doorway with Victoria by his side. She looked at the ground and clung to her purse.

In the elevator, the guard stepped in after them. His finger hovered over the buttons, as if not sure which one he was going to push. Victoria grabbed Jeff's hand and pulled him back on to the floor. "I forgot I'm claustrophobic," she called behind her shoulder, dragging Jeff to the stairway door. "We'll meet you downstairs!"

Without waiting to see what the guard would do, she shoved open the stairway access and dropped his hand. "I don't trust him."

She took the stairs by two, and Jeff matched her pace. "Why are we going upstairs?"

"Shh," she scolded. "I just want to go to the next level and take a different set of stairs down." They rounded the corner and were halfway up the flight when they heard the stairway door behind them. Victoria froze and looked at him wide-eyed. She put a finger on her lips.

He wanted to tell her she was being ridiculous, but he couldn't deny her pleading eyes. He remained still. They heard a few choice words muttered under the guard's breath as his feet slapped the stairs going down, down, down.

Another stairway door slammed. Victoria crept softly back down the stairs. He followed until they had returned to the fourth floor. Her long fingers pressed on the door handle gently, opening the stairway without a sound. She held it open just wide enough for Jeff to slip through before she eased it closed.

"Why are we playing hide-and-seek, Victoria? What if there really is a security problem?"

"Did you notice he wasn't sure what elevator button

to push? Like he was debating where he was going to take us?" She lowered her voice. "I think he's the guy that was following me yesterday. I think he's the one who set my house on fire."

"Are you sure?"

Her eyes widened. "Of course I'm not sure or I'd be the first one calling the police right now. I never saw him that close, but I have a strong feeling."

"We need more than a feeling to go to the police."

She threw her hands up and charged toward his office. "Don't you think I know that?"

"The security breach could be real, Victoria. Let's go."

"Then why didn't he tell us what the security breach was? Don't you think that's a bit odd?"

Jeff rubbed his left temple. He needed more coffee. "Maybe they thought the breach was you?"

"That's ridiculous. I was with you." She jogged into his office and slipped into his desk chair, her wide eyes directed at the computer screen. "No! No, no, no."

"What?"

"Someone is updating or rebooting the entire system right now." She slapped his desk. "I don't know what's going on!"

Jeff walked around to see for himself when a blast boomed so loud it shook the windows. He instinctively stepped closer to Victoria to shield her.

She looked up at him and grabbed his sleeve. "What was that?"

He clenched his jaw. "I'm guessing that was the security breach." Jeff looked toward the elevators and listened closely for any secondary explosions. After a tense moment, he dared to look out his office window. His gut dropped at the sight, and he sagged against the windowsill.

"How bad is it?" Victoria joined him and groaned. "Oh, Jeff."

He shook his head, staring at the shell of his beautiful convertible now covered in flames. It was used and old, but he had paid cash. A drive in that car invigorated him whenever he didn't have time to skydive. He blinked and kicked at the wall underneath the window. That'd teach him to care about possessions…and to stop choosing the highest insurance deductible.

"Look! On the other side of that sedan." Victoria tapped her finger against the glass. He followed her gaze and spotted Charlie crouched down with a walkie-talkie against his cheek. "I'm so relieved he's okay."

Jeff turned to her, focused. "I think it's time to get out of here."

"But the files," she sputtered.

"The reboot is a little too convenient, isn't it? I'm guessing your file is long gone now." He led her across the department floor to a different set of stairs.

She let out a long breath. "You believe me."

"I believe something is going on. I just don't really understand what yet."

She grabbed the stair railing and followed after him. "Where will we go? Your car—"

Jeff frowned but didn't slow down. Surely an idea would come to him by the first floor. He pushed his legs to go faster. Adrenaline always helped clear his mind. Victoria let out a cry, and he jerked to a stop just as she slammed into his back. "Are you okay?"

"I think so. I was trying to keep up and missed a step."

She straightened, and Jeff managed a quick look at

her ankle. It seemed okay, but his gut twisted anyway. He was so focused on the anger from his car being blown up that he wasn't being considerate. His mouth parted as an idea formed. "I know where we're going."

Once they reached the bottom stair, he turned to her. "You sure you're okay?"

"I'm not going to let anything slow me down with that creep trying to find us. Where to?"

"I have a friend that lives near here." His hands hovered over the exit sign on the door. "Stay close to me, okay?"

Victoria tapped his shoulder. "Jeff. Security cameras."

"Then let's hope our security breach friend isn't watching right now." Jeff glanced up briefly, then shoved the door open. Hints of dawn pushed back the darkness enough for Jeff to find his bearings. "We have about four blocks to go before we get to Drake's place."

"Drake?" she said breathlessly. "Who is Drake?"

Victoria raised her chin and pumped her arms to keep up, but her stride seemed more like a hobble.

"You're limping."

"I'm fine."

Her jaw was clenched; she was most definitely not fine. "I wish we could afford to go slower." He offered his arm. "Lean on me."

Victoria bit her lip and shook her head, until her eyes darted to the office building behind them. She took a deep breath, hooked her arm around his biceps, and they pressed forward. Except, he could barely feel her weight on his arm. "Victoria, we won't move faster unless you put your full weight on me."

She grimaced but said nothing. She did, however, lean in closer to him, and he compensated for her slight pull with each step. "Drake is a pilot and a fellow skydiving instructor," Jeff explained. "He does the camera work on all my jumps and vice versa. We used to be roommates until I got my own place."

"Skydiving? Wow. You really are quite the outdoorsman, then."

In a normal situation, Jeff would feel nothing but pride hearing Victoria speak about him in such a way. His identity and dreams all involved the outdoors. The day job was a necessity until he saved enough money, which brought his thoughts back to his car exploding. He'd worked so hard to pay cash for that car. Heat surged through his veins as the reality truly sank in; the fire at Victoria's house couldn't have been an accident either.

He led Victoria in a hurried limp across the property's lawn and into the adjoining subdivision where shadows and large trees would keep them hidden.

Victoria gritted her teeth, trying to will away the searing pain that shot up her shin every time her heel made contact with the ground. If she just had a moment to rest, she was sure the pain would retreat. She tried not to lean too much onto Jeff, but the faster he walked, the more she had to press into his arm.

At least for a brief moment, it was a relief for him to understand the gravity of her situation. But that relief quickly faded with the understanding it was her fault his car was burned to a crisp. His face looked red, and his arm felt rock hard. The man was stressed to be sure, but mostly seemed angry.

Sirens reached her ears as a disorienting dizziness washed over her. She hadn't realized she'd stopped until

Jeff patted the arm she'd wrapped around his elbow. The man's touch was unnerving even amid the circumstances.

"Are you okay?"

Victoria closed her eyes and shook her head. "I'll be fine. It's the second time in hours that I've heard fire trucks coming my way."

"We might be dealing with a pyromaniac."

"Do you think we should've stayed there and waited for the police?"

"If the circumstances were different, I'd say yes. I don't like the thought of what could happen to you before then." Jeff jutted his chin forward. "Except the more I think about it… I'd like to be sure they weren't trying to set you up first."

"Wait. What do you mean?"

Jeff rifled his left hand through his hair. "Think about it. First they cancel your security privileges—your whole account, really—and then they say there's a security breach." He glanced quickly at Victoria. "I'd feel a lot better if we could get that evidence in our hands."

"You and me both." She pulled out her smartphone from her purse. "It's barely past five in the morning. I've got three hours before my FBI appointment."

"Drake is going to kill me," Jeff muttered. She leaned on him as they made their way up the driveway to the left side of a duplex. Jeff rang the doorbell. Headlights rounded the corner from the street leading to Earth Generators. Jeff saw it as well but reacted by pushing Victoria into the shadows with him. "Stay still," he said.

The silver muscle car slowly went down the street. Victoria sagged. "It wasn't the Range Rover."

He nodded, but his eyes stayed focused on the car. "Yeah, but it looks familiar."

Victoria narrowed her eyes. She was no car expert, but it seemed like April had a car like that. "You would know better than me if it's April's or not."

He shifted his focus to Victoria. Their faces were way too close for comfort. He tilted his head like a confused puppy. "I didn't say anything about April." The porch light flipped on, saving her from embarrassment. Victoria held up a hand to shield her eyes. Jeff stepped up to the door and waved at the peephole. "It's me."

The door swung open to reveal a guy in khaki shorts and an olive-green T-shirt. His matted sandy hair hung down over his squinting eyes. "Dude. It's too-early-thirty. What are you doing here? You need a place to crash?"

Victoria stepped onto the patio to join Jeff. Drake's eyes widened at the sight of her. "Well, hello." He swung his head in a motion that flipped his long bangs back.

"We need a ride, Drake. My car—" Jeff closed his eyes a moment, in grief. "Can you drive us back to my place?"

Drake groaned and muttered a few unpleasant words as he shoved on shoes and grabbed his keys, but he didn't ask any questions. What kind of guy had friends who would help him out at five in the morning without any questions asked? Did she even have a friend who would do that?

The backseat of the pickup had very little legroom, but she had it to herself. When would be the next time she would be in a place of her own? Her neighbor Darcy would no doubt let her stay a night or two, but then Victoria would need a place to stay with Baloo while her house was rebuilt. And if she didn't have a job to— Victoria blinked back tears. She couldn't let herself think that way.

Drake pulled into Jeff's assigned space in front of the

set of town house buildings. Looking out the window, Victoria noticed Jeff's front door was open. Thoughts of her dog out in the city propelled her forward. "Baloo!" she shouted and flung the back door open. Disregarding the pain in her ankle, she ran up the stairs toward his door. Two arms grabbed her around the waist.

All the air rushed out of her lungs as her feet left the ground. The arms around her middle loosened, and she turned to find Jeff holding a finger up to his mouth. She tried not to cough, but it was useless. Her lungs were still very sensitive after the night's events. Victoria glared at him. "Baloo," she croaked.

"You can't just walk in there. Someone might still be inside." Jeff pointed hard at his front door. "Go back to the truck with Drake," he whispered.

"Then you shouldn't go in there either!"

The outburst made her lungs spasm again, and a series of coughs prompted Jeff to put both hands on her arms.

"You okay?"

"What if the guy bombs your place like he bombed your car?" she asked, careful not to strain her voice.

Jeff straightened to his full height, several inches above her. "I hadn't thought of that." He pulled out his phone and dialed the police. "Hopefully they caught the creep that blew up my car by now, and this will just add to his sentence."

She didn't take her eyes off the door. "What if there is more than one creep?"

Jeff's jaw clenched. He offered her his free arm and marched her back down to the truck. He took her behind it and around to the other side, the farthest distance away from his ajar town house door. Just as she worried he was going to force her back into the tiny backseat, she heard a growl. Jeff's arm dropped as he turned and found Baloo giving him the evil eye.

"Baloo!" Victoria dropped to one knee and let her dog snuggle up into her arms.

Drake watched from behind the steering wheel, his window rolled down. "Guess your stalker dude likes dogs more than cars."

Victoria stood, her jaw clenched. "Please don't compare a hunk of metal to a hero."

"A hero?"

"Baloo saved my life last night."

"Seriously?" Drake nodded appreciatively. "I totally respect that."

She drew in a deep breath, hoping to regain control of her emotions. "I didn't mean to snap at you." A small square of fabric hung from Baloo's bottom lip. She reached down and removed the denim from his lower canine tooth. "Besides, I don't think he let Baloo go by choice." She ruffled his fur. "Good dog."

Jeff missed her interchange with Drake as he spoke rapidly into the phone.

Baloo stood directly at her side, practically on her foot. She looked over her shoulder to confirm they were still alone. They were safe, for now.

Baloo left her side, approached Jeff and pressed into his leg. Jeff patted Baloo's head while he answered questions on the phone. Huh. Baloo must've decided Jeff was all right. She blinked hard. It was a good thing Jeff was off-limits, because her heart was getting harder to guard.

Her neck tingled as if someone was watching her. She turned to find Drake looking between her and Jeff with a goofy grin on his face. She shook her head but wasn't willing to talk about the reasons why a relationship would never work.

Drake's head bobbed to the seventies music playing softly on the radio. Was he disagreeing with her, or truly enjoying the music? She racked her brain, trying to think of something to say to ease the awkwardness. "So, you skydive with Jeff?"

"Yeah." He yawned. "We met in the Earth Generators factory like ten years ago. I watched him work his way out of there, but he didn't leave me behind. Dude's got a heart of gold. He got me started on this skydiving business. Jeff's got some big plans, which means big plans for me, you know?" Drake looked forward out the window. "I'm better off for knowing him."

Victoria blinked. A heart of gold?

Her next question froze on the tip of her tongue at the sight of police cars and a black armored van surrounding them.

FOUR

It seemed as if a lifetime passed while they waited for the bomb squad to do a sweep of his apartment and Victoria's car. That hour wasn't spent twiddling thumbs, though. Jeff endured a lecture from a tall, burly officer. He lost count of how many times the man said, "You left the scene?"

"As I said before, I believed we were in danger and didn't think it was prudent to wait around for the cops to show up."

The officer launched into reasons why that was a "false" assumption. "You should have called. You made our job harder. Now, explain again why you thought you were in danger, because according to the initial report, malfunction of the engine was listed as a possible cause."

Jeff's mouth fell open. "You've got to be kidding me."

The officer raised an eyebrow. "Vehicle fires account for 16 percent of fire department responses, sir. The fire started with the engine, emergency response vehicles were called, but unfortunately, the fire reached the gas tank before they arrived. So I'm going to repeat my question: Why did you think you were in danger?"

Jeff answered, but kept getting distracted by what

was happening twenty feet away—on the other side of the parking lot—another officer was questioning Victoria. Jeff's gut churned as he watched her. What had made him think he could be a hero? If Victoria's theory proved to be wrong, then both of their jobs would be on thin ice. Only, after they found out about his past, he wouldn't be of any help.

A commotion at the end of the building, at Victoria's car, caught the officer's attention. He fiddled with his earpiece a moment, then cleared his throat. "Sir, we will be looking more closely at your car. They just found explosives in your friend's vehicle."

Jeff fought a wave of nausea. So the man in the baseball cap had placed an explosive in her car, checked his apartment out, then followed him to the office and put an explosive in his car? How was that possible? "We're dealing with more than one person," he said aloud.

The officer didn't appear to hear him as he spoke into his radio.

Jeff raised his voice to get the officer's attention. "If the same explosive was set in my car as her car, why did mine go off first? Why hasn't hers gone off? Do you have to turn on the car for it to explode?"

The policeman pursed his lips and lifted his eyes to the skies. "I'm not an explosives expert, but my understanding is the type of blasting material used is very temperamental." He shrugged. "A stray cat, a squirrel, a strong vibration of a truck passing…you should be glad we found this one before it came to that."

Across the parking lot, Victoria sat on the curb of the road, one arm around Baloo and one hand on her forehead. Jeff wanted to be with her when they broke the news about the bomb. Only a couple of hours ago she'd voiced the worry that someone wanted her dead, and he hadn't believed her. Would any of this have been avoided if he had? The policeman assigned to her was speaking rapidly. No doubt, giving her the same lecture Jeff had just received about leaving the scene.

An hour later, the officer finally gave Jeff the okay to go into his town house. No explosives were found inside. He prayed they hadn't missed anything. Taking the stairs, Jeff hoped his intruders hadn't been there to rob. With his car gone, his mountain bike was his only mode of transportation, and they better have left it untouched.

What if the intruder had discovered the fire safe he kept underneath a spare blanket? The safe contained not only his important documents but also his stash of emergency cash, a total of two thousand dollars. Thanks to Uncle Dean, Jeff didn't believe in banks for emergency uses. Emergency cash needed to be accessed in a heartbeat, not after a long line during bank business hours. It had taken Jeff a year and a half to save his emergency funds before he thought it prudent to start squirreling away toward his dream business. The seed money for that, at least, was tucked away in a savings account.

An officer walked out of his front door as Jeff took the last step onto the landing. "So far we're under the impression that nothing was stolen. You want to confirm that before we leave?" The officer stepped back into the apartment, allowing Jeff enough room to slip through the doorway.

Sounds of footsteps behind him prompted a look over his shoulder. Drake followed him into the living room and slapped a hand on his shoulder while the officer beside Jeff wrote on a tablet. "Dude! This is nuts. They didn't even have the decency to learn how to pick a lock. Your door is messed up, man."

A glance confirmed Drake's proclamation. Shards of wood splayed out from around the lock. Jeff knew what he'd be doing the rest of the day. A new door wasn't cheap or fun to install, not to mention a new doorknob and a strong bolt would be on the list. He turned around and nodded at the officer. "Did they get any other apartments, too?"

"So far, just yours," Drake answered. "That's what the dude downstairs said." Drake held up a finger. "I'm getting a phone call. Hello? Yeah, you got my text? Can you believe it?"

No, Jeff couldn't believe it. His friend seemed to be enjoying the drama. He needed to instruct Drake to stop spreading the news among his friends. Jeff wasn't even sure if he was telling people that Jeff knew personally, but the officer interrupted his intention. "Sir, we need you to check your room."

Jeff followed the directive but still burned with curiosity. He entered his room with apprehension. Everything looked different, but he couldn't pinpoint anything wrong. Perhaps it was simply the knowledge that a stranger had invaded his privacy. The navy comforter lay smooth, just as he had left it that morning. He fingered the top of the red oak dresser. Jeff had made the piece of furniture when he was seventeen years old. He knew where every nick and sloppy corner could be found within its four drawers. His comb and the small basket where he kept unrecorded receipts still sat in the middle, seemingly untouched.

He flung open the closet and breathed a sigh of relief. Underneath the thick comforter, folded neatly on the ground, sat his fire safe, untouched.

"They take your television?" The officer jotted notes on his clipboard.

"Uh, no. I don't own a TV."

The officer tilted his head. "Then they were after computers. I'll need the make and model."

Jeff spun around. "I did have a laptop. Left it in the living room."

"Yeah, that's gone." The officer blinked slowly and then looked around the room. "Okay, so we know what they were after."

Drake groaned, somehow having caught the tail end of the conversation. "That had all our skydiving video footage on it, didn't it? Our clients are gonna freak."

Jeff stared at the carpet. First, his car, now his laptop; it would take a long time to save up that kind of money again after paying the insurance deductibles.

"Are you sure that's all?" the cop asked. Jeff followed the officer's gaze around his room. With nothing on the walls, he supposed it did look bare bones to most. But the simplicity of his decor gave him plenty of room to do his morning stretching exercises before running or biking.

"Everything seems to be here," Jeff acknowledged.

The officer nodded, and Jeff followed him back into the living room. Drake bumped into his shoulder, texting. "Drake!" Jeff often felt he needed to compete with Drake's phone to have even the shortest of conversations. "What are you doing?"

"Texting what they took. Your computer. And that big batch of beef jerky you made yesterday. I only got to eat one piece. That was your best batch yet, and pretty pricey to make, too. Primo beef, man."

Jeff rolled his eyes. "Thanks for noticing, Drake."

"What flavor?" the cop asked.

"Jalapeño," Drake answered for him.

The officer shook his head, jotting notes. "Animals."

Drake held his hands out toward the officer. "This is what I'm saying. Thank you."

Another officer walked into the apartment with Victoria at his side. "You done here?" With an official nod, the second officer directed Victoria to the couch in the living room.

"We need to ask you both a few questions."

Jeff sank into his couch next to Victoria. Except, he felt anything but comfortable. Her eyes were brighter than usual, as if she'd been crying. He wanted to give her a hug, but it didn't seem appropriate, and he got the sense she didn't want any comfort from him. Victoria had always seemed to have an invisible wall up whenever they had a conversation at work, but it appeared the wall had grown stronger. He grimaced. She had come to him for help, and he hadn't been able to fix anything.

The police interrupted his thoughts once more with their questions. He listened as Victoria repeated all that had happened over the past twenty-four hours. She included all her suspicions at work, and that's when Jeff saw it. Skepticism was written all over the officers' faces. Victoria turned her gaze to the ceiling.

"Why didn't you take your suspicion to the FBI?" the lead officer pressed.

"I made an appointment for this morning," she said, meekly. "Clearly none of this would've happened if I had insisted they see me yesterday, but it was almost after hours and wasn't an emergency."

"Who's the appointment with?" the second officer asked.

"Agent Doug Brunson."

The officer stood and pointed at her. "Make sure you get to that appointment."

As the officer walked away a large hand slapped onto his shoulder. "I'm glad you're okay." Jeff looked up to see Drake hovering. "I guess there are some benefits to being poor, if all they took was a laptop."

He crossed his arms over his chest. Why'd Drake have to say stuff like that in front of Victoria? "I'm not poor, Drake. I choose to put my money elsewhere."

"How about you use that money to call us in some Chinese food, then? I'll wait here while you run to the hardware store."

"It's only nine in the morning," Jeff responded, but his stomach betrayed him by choosing that moment to growl.

"See what I'm saying?" Drake pointed at Jeff while he walked backward to his kitchen. "I'll find us some grub." Drake's phone vibrated, and he automatically answered. "Yeah, Dude. Bomb squad and everything."

Jeff felt an ache develop in the back of his neck. Drake had more people to call about the burglary than Jeff. Sure, his phone was full of contacts, but no one was close enough he'd feel comfortable calling to tell them about his morning. Why would someone break into the apartment for a measly laptop and nothing else? He never took home files from Earth Generators. Victoria remained silent and rhythmically stroked Baloo's back.

He took it as his cue to speak up. "I think they took the laptop because they thought I might have the evidence on it."

She nodded. "I figured as much."

"That's why I'm coming to the FBI appointment with you."

Her whole body straightened as if a heavy burden had just been lifted off her shoulders. "Really? You would do that for me?" She looked at Baloo. "I haven't slept since probably one in the morning. I'm dragging and can't think straight. Do you think we can swing by and get some coffee on the way to the Federal Building?"

Jeff laughed. "I think we could both use it. After this morning, we're going to have to be on the lookout the entire way there."

Victoria desperately wanted to close her eyes. "You sure Drake will be fine?" She checked the side mirror several times with each block. "It was nice of him to let us borrow his truck…especially given the circumstances."

"Drake may come across as goofy, but believe it or not, the guy's a genius. No doubt he's worked up a plan by now. Besides, Drake makes friends wherever he goes. You heard him—he had that officer in the palm of his hand. When we left, they were talking about starting a beef jerky business together. Using my recipes." Jeff laughed. "Hopefully, the officer will see reason after dropping Drake off. Besides, Drake has another car at his place."

"You're a chef, too?" she interjected. An image of cooking dinner shoulder to shoulder in his kitchen assaulted her imagination. If ever there were a job description for the perfect man for her, on paper, Jeff would qualify. And yet, she knew all too well that made him more of a risk.

"I dabble. Mostly a few signature dishes to feed myself and not much more."

She put a hand on her forehead. Over and over in her mind's eye she could see her car burst into flames. It never had, of course, thanks to the SWAT team and Jeff's fast thinking, but it could've happened so easily. Victoria pointed to the closest strip mall. "They have a drive-through. I just need a moment to process all of this before the meeting."

Jeff looked in the rearview mirror. "Did you see any glimpse of that Rover?"

She dug her fingers into the fabric upholstery on either side of her legs. "No. But that doesn't mean much anymore, does it? If someone is willing to set your house on fire or bomb your car to kill you, surely they have the means to find a different vehicle."

Jeff pulled the truck directly into the drive-through lane of her favorite coffee shop, The Groovy Bean. "Baloo seems comfy in the backseat."

Victoria took a look for herself. Sure enough, Baloo was practically snoring in the backseat. He took up the entire length of the bench. "I feel the same way, buddy," she mumbled.

They were second in line to be waited on, but Jeff's constant sweeping of the area set her nerves on edge. He scratched his chin where a five-o'clock shadow had begun to form. She'd never seen him with facial hair before. She supposed he usually shaved in the morning—another reminder that she was interfering with his life. Although, she wondered what he would look like with a beard. Probably just as attractive, if not more.

He raised an eyebrow, and for a brief moment Victoria was worried she'd said her thoughts aloud.

"If they really wanted to kill us, why not shoot us?"

Victoria cringed. She didn't want to acknowledge guns were a real possibility. "Maybe they wanted it to look like an accident?"

"No, I don't think so. You can trace bomb materials."

She stared at Jeff, letting her mind run. "What if the bomb was to get Charlie out of the building, so they could lure us somewhere else?"

"To kill us a different way?" Jeff scowled. "That's what makes me nervous. I don't think they care so much about making it look like an accident. Fires? Bombs?" He shook his head. "No, I don't think that's why guns haven't been a part of this. I doubt they would try anything again at my place now, though. There's already evidence of a break-in."

"I'm relieved we're not dealing with snipers, or we might not be having this conversation." Victoria peeked at the time on her smartphone. "You need time to fix your door today. And maybe you should install an alarm system." Victoria reached for her wallet. "Fat lot of good that did me, though."

"You had an alarm system at your house?"

She nodded. "Yep. My brother set that one up, too. Same sort of thing as the car alarm, but I couldn't afford the big bucks for security cameras, and clearly whoever started the fire didn't need access inside to light a match."

He waved away her money. "This is my treat." He pulled up to the sign with coffee choices. "On our way, let's make sure we're on the same page before you start talking to that agent. We need to give them every reason to take us seriously."

"Especially without a lick of evidence."

"Exactly why it's time to bring out the big guns. I'm thinking a triple shot espresso. You?"

Victoria laughed. The sensation felt so foreign. Jeff grinned, and she couldn't help but notice his eyes were deep brown—like dark chocolate—and her weakness for cocoa ran deep. "Chocolate," she murmured.

He cocked his head. "Mocha, then?"

Her cheeks heated. "I'm not sure," she stammered. "I'll have what you're having."

Jeff handed her the largest salted caramel latte that money could buy and a side order of coffee cake. She allowed herself to enjoy Jeff's company for the briefest of moments. The man was the epitome of handsome. His sun-kissed skin, the way the navy in his shirt made his eyes look darker, his thick wavy hair...

Jeff set his latte down a little too hard on the console between them, the small splash of liquid snapping her out of her daydream. His cheeks flushed. "Sorry. I got lost in my thoughts."

She took a sip of coffee to hide her smile. Had he just caught himself thinking of her, too? Victoria's mind flashed to her ex-boyfriend, Blake, a guy who was seemingly perfect on the outside—handsome, kind, funny and successful. Yet, if Victoria had ever acted as if he wasn't the perfect man at all times, he'd flirt with the very next woman that crossed his path. Jeff wouldn't do something like that—she was positive his integrity wouldn't permit it—but she was also confident from what the ladies at work had told her that Jeff had major commitment issues. It was the reminder she needed to keep her thoughts in check. Besides, April made it clear she had her eyes set on him, so she needed to put Jeff out of her mind once and for all.

He set the truck in Drive. "I keep going over what you've told me, Victoria, and I have to say, if I put myself in Wagner's shoes, I'd be upset you brought a personal flash drive into work." He held up a hand. "Don't get me wrong, Wagner didn't handle it well. But while he reacted inappropriately, that doesn't necessarily mean he's the mastermind behind all of this."

It was as if Jeff had just punched her in the gut. Whatever temptation she'd ever had to think of him in a romantic light disappeared completely. "It was a company-issued flash drive, thank you very much." She pointed firmly at the center of the console, as if the drive were physically there in front of them. "I have every right to transport files for work-related use. In fact, feel free to go ahead and quiz me, Mr. Tucker. You'll find that I know the employee handbook backward and forward. I did nothing that crosses ethical boundaries or even violates company policy."

Jeff's features softened. "I didn't mean to put you on the defensive, Victoria. I was trying to see the situation from every angle." He sighed. "Wagner used to be a man I respected. I've been to his house in the foothills before." He focused intently on the stoplight in front of him. "Up until now, I've always imagined him to be a man of professional integrity."

"Professional integrity?"

Jeff shrugged. "I don't know anything about his personal life. I heard rumors about a rich wife, but that's just hearsay. He lives in a beautiful minimansion, but there weren't any family photographs. Although, to be fair, it isn't that out of the ordinary—my family never hung up any photographs either."

Victoria traced the lid of her cup. "Sounds odd to me.

I don't think I've been in a family's home that hasn't had photographs on display."

He tilted his head from side to side. "Well, I acknowledge that my family is a bit odd."

Victoria wanted to ask a follow-up question about his family but wanted to avoid anything personal.

Jeff rubbed his chin. "Okay, forget Wagner. Let me try to think like the FBI will. Why didn't you go to the audit committee when you first suspected something amiss?"

"The audit committee? The one made of board members?"

"Yes."

"I think you just answered your own question. We don't have a whistle-blower policy in place and—"

"Victoria, it's federal law. You can't be penalized if you—"

"You don't need to tell me that, Jeff. I'm an accountant." She took a deep breath. He'd asked her not to get defensive, and instead she snapped at him. If she wanted to keep him on her side, she needed to tame the emotional roller coaster. "There is no policy in place that allows employees to contact the board members without getting the attention of other people who might be behind fraud."

"Because you have to go through the chain of command to contact the board members," he mused aloud. Jeff tapped his fingers on the steering wheel. "If you're right, then what makes you think the board isn't behind this?"

"Have you seen the list of members? They're all former presidents of Fortune 500 companies. Not a single one of them would need to risk jail to get the kind of money we're talking." She pointed to her red purse. "Our management team has more motive. The CEO, CFO, COO…"

"We have way too many COs."

"And four vice presidents," she finished. "They could easily have a hand in this, but I think this type of fraud would require a department head on the inside to get the job done. Someone like Wagner."

Victoria's phone buzzed. She glanced at it. "That's my reminder alarm. My appointment is in fifteen minutes. How far away is the Federal Building?"

He put a hand on his chest. "I believe you, but I didn't get a chance to look at the report long enough to fully corroborate your story. So, if the authorities aren't willing to give you protection tonight, I think you better plan to stay at a hotel."

"Oh, but my neighbor—"

"Your neighbor is too easy to target. Just like you were in your house. I think you should get some cash from an ATM. Then you can stay at a hotel, without credit cards."

She closed her eyes. What kind of hotel would let you check in with cash? A dive, that's what. A yawn escaped her. An unbidden image of her home, then her bedroom, flashed in her mind. She took another sip of coffee and closed her eyes to keep the tears from escaping. She cleared her throat. "What about you? They know where you live now." Her breath shuddered. Also her fault.

"I might stay at a friend's or do the same as you. We'll see how this meeting goes."

Victoria mentally calculated the cost of a hotel. Thankfully, payday had only been last Friday. Yet she couldn't count on getting a paycheck next week if her job was in question. Jeff took a sharp turn to the right, then did another visual sweep.

He pointed ahead. "An ATM." He drove into the entrance of the drive-up ATM the wrong way so that Victoria would be within arm's reach of the machine. She leaned out the window, slid in the bank card and entered the security code. It'd be wise to double-check her balance before cashing out a large amount. By now, all her monthly scheduled bill payments should've been withdrawn. She pressed the button to see her balance. Her mouth went dry. The numbers on the screen were shocking: $257,420.

She flung a hand to her mouth. How? A burning in the pit of her stomach prompted her eyes to well with tears. Whoever was behind the fraud—behind the fire and explosion—had done this. How would anyone believe her now? She couldn't face the FBI with nothing but seeming proof that she was the culprit, the embezzler.

She sank back down into her seat and dropped her head into her hands.

FIVE

Jeff looked out in the street in hopes of giving Victoria privacy. A man wearing a baseball cap approached the bank on the adjacent sidewalk. While he was the same height as the security guard, he didn't have the same slope to his shoulders. The guy turned, and Jeff studied his eyes. Nope, definitely not him. But why was he looking so keenly at Victoria?

Jeff turned to find Victoria crumpled in her seat. "Victoria! Are you okay? Did something hit you?" He flung off his seat belt and took her hand, feeling for her pulse. It bounced rapidly against his fingers, but at least it was there. "What happened? Can you breathe?" He looked at her coffee cup in alarm. Was she poisoned?

Victoria shook her head fiercely. Her face had lost all color.

Maybe the stress and the lack of sleep had fully caught up to her?

She raised a shaky hand and pointed to the ATM. He released her wrist and squinted. He looked back and forth between Victoria and the screen.

"I take it that's not the correct balance."

"What am I going to do? They're trying to set me up. They…they can't kill me, so instead they frame me?"

"Or worse. They want to do both." Like it or not, he was part of this now. Assuming they wanted both of them dead, wouldn't they want both of them framed, as well? Jeff slipped out of the truck and walked around to the machine. He inserted his own bank card. Willing himself to stay calm, he pushed the required numbers into the keypad and prayed for a normal balance.

$301,470.

Jeff slapped both sides of the machine in frustration. Why? The amount put into his account was even bigger. Jeff closed his eyes, trying to will away the urge to smash the bank machine for betraying him. But he couldn't lose his temper any more than he already had, or Victoria would think he was mad at her. And while there was a small part of him that was furious, he knew logically it wasn't her fault.

He grew livid with Wagner, if in fact, his boss was at all responsible for any of this. And he was mad at the Lord. Why would He allow this? Specifically this?

No one would believe Jeff's innocence if they knew of his past. Hadn't he repented fully, led a good moral life and done what he thought God asked of him? He'd turned around one-hundred-eighty degrees both in attitude and action.

"Jeff, what is it?"

He heard Victoria slip out of the truck and stand behind him, but he didn't turn to face her. She looked over his shoulder at the screen and groaned. "No, not you, too. I'm so sorry for dragging you into this. Jeff, I had no idea. I never intended—" her voice cracked.

Instinct relaxed Jeff's muscles enough to pull Victoria into a hug. He wouldn't be able to handle it if she started crying. *Please, Lord, don't let her cry.* He'd grown up an only child in a family that didn't show affection. He didn't know how to deal with crying women. *It'd be the last straw, Lord. Please, help her keep it together.* "It's going to be okay," he mumbled. He felt a drop of moisture on his chest. *Oh, no.*

"You've been so nice." She sniffed. "I just wanted to help people, and instead my house and your car—" She stepped out of his embrace. "I need to tell you something. This isn't the first time something like this has happened to me." She held up her hands. "No, not getting framed or…or hunted. I meant it's not the first time I've found tampered reports. At the last company I worked for, I reported my findings, but when my claims were investigated they found nothing…and I was asked to resign."

Awareness hit Jeff in the gut. "That's why you didn't report the discrepancies when you first saw them. That's why you waited for evidence this time." He exhaled when she nodded.

"And for the final icing on the cake, we're either going to end up dead or in jail. You know that, right?" Her hands moved to her face. "I don't know what to do." Her words were muffled, but he still heard them. And the truth was he didn't know either.

"We pray." The words came out of his mouth stiff and cross, but his heart felt a twinge. It was the certainty that came with knowing he was doing the right thing. He lifted his face to the sky in prayer. *Lord, what do we do? Help, please.* There was one place that he felt closest to God. An idea quickly formed in his mind.

He lowered his chin to find Victoria's eyes wet with tears but stunningly beautiful. Were her eyes always that blue? The vulnerable way she looked up at the sky took him off guard. "You're right," she whispered, and he felt a surge of courage.

His gaze dropped down to her lips. How could he be irritated, concerned and attracted all at the same time to a crying woman? He took a step back. "I have an idea, but it's going to require a lot of trust on your part."

"I thought we were going to pray."

He nodded. "I did."

She raised an eyebrow. "I assumed you meant we were going to pray together."

If they started praying together, wouldn't that indicate intimacy? Especially after he'd hugged her? One of his strengths as supervisor was the ability to redirect. He smiled. "Better get back in the truck. We're not safe in the open."

She rolled her eyes and got in the truck. Where was the appreciative woman from a second ago? "Want to hear my idea?"

He started to back up the truck before she said, "Sure." Her expression didn't match her words.

"I know a place we can go—and more important, a way we can go—that's off the radar. There would be no way for anyone to follow us. It'll give us a little time to figure out how to prove ourselves innocent and, hopefully, gather evidence while we're at it."

She tilted her head. "What's the catch?"

Jeff pulled out his phone. "I'll explain on the way. First, we need to stop by my place to get some emergency cash. I don't think we should take any of the money they put in the account."

She lifted her chin. "Of course not! I would never take their money!"

"Do you have that FBI agent's email?"

Victoria lifted her purse and began fumbling inside it. "Yes, I think it's on his business card."

"Okay. I'll drive while you email him on your smartphone. Let him know you can't make the appointment but you're working to find the evidence he needs to proceed."

"Don't mention the money?"

Jeff mentally debated his answer for a moment. "No. I'm guessing that's what the real embezzlers want us to do. If they know us at all, they know both of us are pretty honest to a fault."

Victoria cringed. "I do have the reputation of being a goody-goody, don't I?"

"If you're referring to the banning to-go coffee cups campaign you started, then, yes."

"It wasn't a boycott. I simply wanted us to switch to real mugs or recyclable paper cups like these." She put held up the to-go cup from the coffee shop. "We work at an earth-friendly company, it made sense to do the same in break rooms. Is that so unreasonable? And what about you? You encouraged the staff to voluntarily give up an hour or two of vacation annually to account for long restroom breaks or running five minutes late from lunch."

"That's called being a good supervisor. There's nothing wrong with that."

She laughed. "That's not how your fellow employees saw it. You have more vacation built up than anyone else in the department. It's no sweat off your back to lose a few hours."

"How do you know that?"

Her cheeks flushed. "I've never taken a day off either, but you've worked there more years than me and you're never gone. I did the math."

Jeff wanted to ask her what else she had noticed about

him and why she was embarrassed, but he figured now wasn't the time. "Well, you've proved my point. We have a reputation. Whoever set us up will assume our first move would be to expose the transaction immediately. But instead, let's do the opposite and stay quiet and hidden until we find some evidence to prove our innocence."

"Agreed. If only I had more time. I feel like there's something I'm missing—some clue—but my thoughts seem jumbled up in a fog." Victoria sighed. "But I don't know, Jeff. I'm worried, wherever we go, we'll be at risk."

"Where we're going, they can't follow."

"Jeff?" She looked up from her smartphone. "What do you mean?"

"A pilot has to file a flight plan, but he doesn't necessarily have to reveal where skydivers leave the plane."

"Jeff." She slapped her hand down on her purse. "What are you saying?"

"Did I already mention that I'm a skydiving instructor on the side?"

They pulled into a parking lot in front of a tin warehouse adjacent to the airport. She closed her eyes. Were they really going to do this?

"I think we should lock your purse in here. Either that, or you can try to squeeze it into my locker inside."

Her eyes flashed open. "I can't bring it with me? You don't have a backpack?"

Jeff swung open the driver-side door and put one foot on the pavement. "I can find a way to take your essentials, but that's it."

Victoria pulled her red bag close. She'd had the purse for five years. It was just the right size to look stylish with its shiny faux-leather material but big enough to fit in all the necessities, including a touch-up cosmetics bag, a travel hairbrush, a container of trail mix, a water bottle and a book for those times she needed to sit and wait. Now she'd have to leave it all behind? She could sense Jeff's disapproval before she turned to see his frown. "I know it seems shallow to you, but this is literally all I have left of my possessions. Everything else went up in flames."

"I don't think you're shallow. I'm sorry I don't have a better idea."

"I appreciate what you're doing. I'm running on fumes, though, so I'm having a hard time not getting emotional." She spun around to the backseat where her dog still dozed. "What about Baloo? My neighbor can't handle big dogs, and Baloo hasn't had a Bordetella vaccine this year, so he can't go to a kennel."

"I made arrangements on my cell when I ran into my apartment. As long as you're fine with Drake watching him for a few days, we're set. I can guarantee he'll take good care of him."

She rubbed the back of her neck to ease the developing knot. "Is this really the only way?"

Jeff rubbed his forehead. "You need rest, and we both need time to figure out how to prove our innocence without fear of being killed. I don't know any other scenario that doesn't risk us being followed."

She frowned. "You still haven't told me where we're going."

"It's not that far away. Just past the foothills." He sighed. "My relatives live off the grid. We don't share the same last name. I never talk about them. We can't be traced there. They have a lot of land, and I know the perfect spot where we can land without people noticing."

So far, Victoria liked the sound of it. The prospect of rest sounded so enticing. Bone-weary, she couldn't stop daydreaming about a bed with plush pillows and a soft quilt. The way she started crying on Jeff's shoulder was evidence of her exhaustion. Would he still take her seriously, or would he start treating her like she was less intelligent, the way Blake had the moment she showed emotion?

"I can make arrangements for a vehicle to be waiting for us where we land." He tapped his hand on the steering wheel.

She sighed. "I don't mean to be causing so much trouble—"

"From now on, you don't apologize. This was premeditated. We were targets, I'm sure of it."

"What are you saying?"

"Victoria, what do you know about direct deposits?"

She pursed her lips, trying to follow his train of thought. She gasped. "They take a minimum of twenty-four hours to complete."

"Exactly. Those deposits had to be planned. Don't you see? They were out to get both of us, Victoria. I'm sure of it. I should be thanking you for coming to me when you did. Any later, and I would've been blindsided. So no apologies." He grinned, and she couldn't help but smile in return. "Okay?"

She nodded, overwhelmed with the truth of his words. "We're in this together."

Rousing instrumental music hit her ears as they walked into the entrance of Airborne Escapades. It seemed more like an airplane hangar than an office building. The counter at the front and the tall portable dividers staged at equal intervals indicated it'd only been slightly modified to house a skydiving school. Jeff beckoned her and Baloo to follow him into a small office. A flat-screen television playing a captioned instructional video grabbed her attention.

"It goes on a loop." He put his hands in his pockets and watched the footage of the skies for a brief moment. "I suggest you watch as much as you can while I make some more arrangements. We don't have the time to go through the usual routine. We'll be set to go in just a few minutes."

Victoria took a seat in one of the uncomfortable metal folding chairs and tried to concentrate on what the narrator was saying. Instead she fought a wave of chills. A rush of fear made her want to throw up.

Jeff may have prayed for both of them, but she didn't feel as though she'd prayed nearly enough. The moment her eyes closed, she remembered the notes she made in her prayer journal from the previous day. *I need to choose to have faith despite feelings of fear.*

Victoria spun in her chair to see Jeff approach in his skydiving jumpsuit and aviator sunglasses. He produced a grin that showed off his white teeth.

"Are you feeling nervous?"

"I think that's an understatement," she answered.

He pulled his glasses off and narrowed his eyes. "Over three million people went skydiving last year. Out of that, there were, tragically, nineteen deaths, but that still makes it safer than driving a car…or walking your dog." He straightened. "Besides, as a licensed instructor, I will do all the worrying for you. I know what I'm doing, Victoria. I wouldn't suggest this if I weren't sure it was safe."

Victoria's heart raced. Nineteen deaths? That was supposed to be reassuring? She sighed dramatically. "You're certified and up-to-date?"

He raised his right hand in a three-fingered oath. "Yes, ma'am. I'll take you on a tandem flight. We'll fly to an altitude of about thirteen-thousand feet, free-fall about fifty seconds, then the parachute will do the rest of the work."

Fifty seconds. Only fifty seconds of flying? In theory, it sounded like a piece of cake. Victoria stood and glanced down at her neighbor's clothes. "Just tell me what I need to do. I'm not sure these clothes are the best suited for—"

Jeff laughed. "Good point." He guided her back into the open warehouse space. She held up a hand to shield her eyes from the bright rays and understood why he already had on his sunglasses. A large sliding door that would allow planes to drive indoors was wide open. "Not the most secure place, is it?" She imagined the man with the red car being able to stride right in at any time. She reached down and rubbed Baloo's fur. Leaving him for even an hour was going to be hard after all that had happened.

"I suppose you're right. But as soon as we get in the air, we won't need to worry about that."

"Victoria! Nice to see you again so soon."

Behind Jeff, she could see Drake in a leather jacket strutting their way.

Jeff looked over his shoulder. "I assume you remember Drake? He'll be our pilot."

She smiled in acknowledgment, but try as she might, she couldn't get the smile to reach her eyes. Jeff gave

Drake a hearty slap on the back. "We'll be ready in just a moment."

"Cool." Drake turned his attention to her. "Jeff and I worked it all out. Your dog will be totally set with Hector, by the way. He loves animals."

"Hector?"

"He works behind the counter. He'll watch him while I'm flying, then I'll take care of Baloo when I get back. I'll treat him like he was my own."

She studied the concrete at her feet, trying to move past the temptation to argue. She was leaving Baloo in a stranger's hands, and she hated it, but knew there was no other option. "Thank you so much for watching him." She waved at Jeff. "And for helping both of us."

"It's all good." He nodded and pulled out a dog treat from his pocket. "Hector has a Great Dane at home and had some organic pumpkin treats in his car. That okay?"

Baloo instantly sat at attention. "Sure," Victoria answered. "I think that's a yes. And you'll need to brush him every day and make sure he has enough food and water at all times and—"

"No prob. I've worked with this breed before," Drake interrupted.

"You—you have?"

Drake fed Baloo another treat. "Yeah, I used to walk dogs back in the day."

Victoria saw Jeff nodding. "You knew that?"

He shrugged. "Yeah. We were roommates."

She eyed Jeff for a moment. Why couldn't he have mentioned that tidbit before? Then it hit her—Jeff was treating her like a supervisor would, even in this situation. He was making the decisions and the arrangements without consulting her. She warred between annoyance and relief that someone else was in charge. Except, if she was going to trust him, they needed to treat each other like equals. Drake walked back and high-fived a man at the counter. "I assume that's Hector?"

"He's a really great guy. So is Drake, for that matter."

She was about to be a passenger in Drake's plane. Her throat went dry. "Okay, but how about his piloting skills?"

"He's certified, Victoria. I trust him with my life all the time."

She gave Baloo a hug. Her mind raced with statistical analysis on the likelihood of seeing Baloo again, the possibility of going to jail or worse. Baloo had saved her, and she didn't want to leave him behind. Jeff cleared his throat, but she didn't move. "I don't suppose you would understand," she said, "but this dog means the world to me."

"No, I understand all too well. I just prefer to not get attached in the first place."

Victoria's eyes narrowed. Yep. She'd almost forgotten. The man was a commitment-phobe, a high risk in the relationship department. Why, April even said—wait, April! She put a hand to her mouth. "What about April?"

"What about her?"

Victoria let out an exasperated sigh. "Won't she be upset if we go on the run together?"

Jeff tilted his head to the side. "Why?"

"Aren't you guys dating?"

Jeff's mouth dropped. "April and I are not dating. What gave you that idea?"

Victoria took a step backward. "What? She told me all about the first date you went on and made it clear to the rest of the office you're off-limits. Which, to be honest, wasn't a big deal, seeing as how you've already dated half of the women on staff."

"What are you talking about?" Jeff scratched his head. "I went out for dinner once with April, months ago. It wasn't a good match, so we agreed to just be friends." He took a deep breath. "And what do you mean I've gone out with half the women at work? I haven't dated a single person in our department. Not that I have to defend myself to you," he added.

"Jeff, come on. Within my first week of work, I had already heard about the Jeff Tucker Dinner Club."

Jeff's eyes widened. "The what?"

"I...I assumed you knew." She softened her tone. "You're kind of known for...you know... Never mind. I probably misheard. So, we're almost ready?"

He moved a step closer and she took a sharp breath. He shook his head. "No, no. You're not getting off that easy. What am I known for?"

She closed her eyes and wished she had kept her mouth closed. "You're kind of known for taking girls out for dinner and then never calling again. A one-date limit, hence the name...the Jeff Tucker Dinner Club."

"There's nothing wrong with taking someone out to dinner to get to know them." He frowned and looked at the floor. "I never imply I'll call. I never make advances. I don't pretend to be romantic. Everyone has been fine to just be friends."

Victoria laughed at his naivety, then coughed at his injured face expression. "I'm sorry. I thought you were aware of your reputation."

"Reputation?"

She studied the partition a few feet in front of them and tried to think of a way out of the awkward conversation. "Guys that typically go out for just one date and nothing more are generally—" she searched for a tactful way to explain "—thought to have a fear of commitment."

Jeff raised an eyebrow and pulled his shoulders back. "I don't expect you to understand, Victoria, but it couldn't be farther from the truth."

His words were weighted, heavy with hidden meaning. She wanted to ask him more, but her cheeks burned. She wished she could run and hide, mortified she ever stuck her foot in her mouth with the one man willing to help her. He and April weren't an item? Why'd April indicate they were?

Her chin dipped to her chest. She couldn't even call April because she didn't have her number. How good a friendship could they have if they didn't exchange numbers? In fact, she only had personal phone numbers from a handful of coworkers, and she couldn't remember ever using them. She rubbed her neck and hoped the sudden heartburn would dissipate as fast as it hit.

Her phone contacts consisted of only her family, book club and church friends—another reminder that she'd been so guarded ever since the humiliation of being asked to resign at her previous job, two years ago.

"I'm not sure we really have time for this discussion, do we?" Jeff asked. His eyes were soft, but his mouth was pursed, his jaw hard.

"Jeff, I didn't mean to offend you," she said gently. He turned with a slight wave as if it was water under the bridge, but her neck still prickled with discomfort. If he wasn't a commitment-phobe then why the reputation of being a one-date guy and why did April lie to her? Perhaps April was projecting her wishful thinking?

With the inspirational music on the speakers cueing her forward, she followed Jeff to the lockers where she would hand over all the possessions she had left in the world. *It's only stuff. Stuff can be replaced.*

Jeff handed her a jumbo-sized fanny pack. "I use this to hold banners for business promotional jumps now and then. It should hold your bare necessities."

She exhaled and slipped her phone and wallet into the fanny pack. When Jeff walked away, she decided to add her cosmetic touch-up case and, at the last second, her pepper spray to the fanny pack contents. "You think my purse is safe in the locker?"

Jeff nodded. "The instructors keep their stuff here, too. The front desk is manned during public hours, as well. You ready to suit up?" He held out a jumpsuit that would zip over her outfit.

She grabbed the blue coveralls. "These do seem more appropriate for flying than my neighbor's clothes."

"So do these." Jeff's hand came around from his back, revealing a pair of sneakers with purple stripes down the side. "It's from another instructor I know. We don't have too many female instructors, but if these don't fit, there is one more pair of shoes in the lost and found."

Victoria imagined Jeff searching to find shoes for her. It was very thoughtful. *Please, let them fit.* She kicked off her neighbor's loafers and slipped on the shoes. They weren't an exact fit, but they weren't so loose to fall off, especially if she tied them tightly enough.

She looked up to find Jeff beaming, clearly proud of himself. Her awareness of his every move heightened as he helped her tighten the harnesses around her body. The very same harness he'd soon connect with his own. She didn't realize she'd have to be so physically close to him. *He does this all the time for clients. I'm just another client.*

The self-talk meant to be a comfort only produced a surge of unexpected jealousy. He had to get up close and personal with plenty of other women. Why was she tortured over this? Even though the likelihood they'd still have their jobs the moment they boarded the plane was slim to nothing, he was still a high risk. Jeff fumbled with her shoulder straps, his eyebrows knit together. He let go and took a step back, his cheeks slightly reddened. "I'm sorry, Victoria. Usually I have Meredith help the female clients and I handle the male ones, but since this was last-minute…" He cleared his throat. "I think it's fairly snug. Make it a little tighter if you want, but it shouldn't cause any pain."

Victoria did as she was told and tried her best not to enjoy the smell his aftershave left behind as he straightened and stepped away. He held out a large laminated sheet with drawings of other people skydiving. "This is all the instruction I get?"

He laughed and transformed into the supervisor she knew. Serious but lighthearted, direct but personable, he launched into a lecture and description of what she would experience. Within a few minutes, she had received a full briefing on what to do during their flight and landing.

Victoria straightened her shoulders. "We better go before I lose my nerve." They made their way out onto the tarmac. Drake held a clipboard and walked around the plane. "What's he looking for?"

"He's doing the final check before takeoff," Jeff explained.

Jeff stepped into the plane first and offered Victoria a hand. She plastered on a smile, despite her fear, accepted his outstretched hand and climbed into the small aircraft. She hadn't realized she was still holding his hand until he squeezed it. "We're going to be okay, Victoria."

Five minutes later, they were rolling down the runway. Drake rattled off numbers and seemingly random words into the headset, and a second later they were in the air. She stared out the window admiring the foothills in the distance.

They that wait upon the Lord shall renew their strength; they shall mount up with wings as eagles; they shall run, and not be weary; and they shall walk, and not faint.

A contented peace washed over her as the verse came to mind. Yet, even with peace, the weariness still remained. *I put my hope in You, Lord.* She saw a bird in the distance. *What does it feel like to soar like an eagle?*

Ten minutes later, Jeff stood up and handed her a pair of goggles. *Never mind, Lord,* she prayed, *I can live life without knowing.* Jeff narrowed his eyes and tapped his head, indicating she needed to follow his example. She sat frozen until he held out his hand. She complied, and he led her to the bar at the open door of the plane. Her mind screamed at her. *Abort! Abort!* She took a step back. What if she accidentally fell out?

A tugging sensation around her middle confirmed that Jeff was in the process of clipping their harnesses together. His arm wrapped around her waist, and his hot breath tickled her ear. "I've got you. Step forward. Cross your arms now."

She closed her eyes and imagined herself as the young, confident woman she used to be, and peace cloaked her. The amount of trust it would take to let go of all anchors to the plane and believe the man behind her would stay true to his word almost made her pass out. She sucked in a deep breath and tucked her chin in just slightly.

Jeff swayed their bodies forward, backward and then forward, right out of the plane.

SIX

Tumbling through the air, Victoria squeezed her eyes shut. Her skin strained against the force of the current as it whipped around her body.

Victoria had screamed on every part of every roller coaster she'd ever ridden—even the flat parts—yet managed to stay quiet as she fell into the open sky. It took every ounce of self-control not to scream, but if she opened her mouth, she feared the oxygen would be sucked from her lungs…or worse, she might inhale a bug. Besides, who would be able to hear her anyway?

The tumbling stopped as suddenly as it had started. She peeked out of one eye first as a test and saw the ground thousands of feet below her, in all of its beauty. A slight movement at her back confirmed that Jeff was following the steps listed on the laminated sheet. He was releasing the drogue chute. In the briefing, he had explained the chute would help them free fall at the same speed as a solo diver.

Jeff's hand tapped the side of her arm, and she obeyed the signal, opening her arms and spreading her legs to help further slow their speed. Jeff's arms brushed against hers, as his long limbs spread out just outside of hers.

The goggles allowed Victoria to truly look around comfortably. She passed a cloud to her right and the next moment could see for miles around. The patterns of green, brown and blue seemed unreal, too perfect. The land was gorgeous!

A sharp tug on her middle took her breath away while her legs simultaneously fell into a vertical position. Victoria caught her breath and smiled. They were floating now so she could really look around. Why had she ever worried? The eagle verse came to her mind again. *Ah, so this is what it feels like, Lord.*

She wanted to stay in the weightless moment when her concerns felt so far away. Someone else was taking care of the journey, and she could just enjoy the ride. Shouldn't that be how she lived her life? It seemed like an easy concept while feeling weightless. Her mind flooded with reality—job, fraud, jail, money—she cringed.

The ground grew closer, and she found herself wishing the dive could last longer. All around her were trees, in every direction. Were they at an orchard or tree farm? She stiffened. Wait. How could they land on top of trees?

Jeff bit his lip. Since when had his uncle planted an orchard? It was too late now to focus on his assumptions and stupidity; he needed to concentrate on getting them out of the situation. He fought to pull the steering toggles to the far right. There was no time to process. Out of one danger zone and into the next, his mind raced through his maneuver training. They couldn't safely land here.

He kicked forward with all his strength, sending Victoria's legs up. He bent his knees, in an attempt to catch her legs on top of his. Thankfully, she didn't fight the movement and pulled her legs up to her chest, as well.

The maneuver swept them past the rows and rows of trees. Jeff shifted the parachute slightly to speed them up but that would sacrifice their soft landing, so he backed off slightly. *Please, help her remember what to do, Lord.* He steeled his sights on a clear spot in preparation for landing.

At the sight of the ground approaching, she stuck her legs out, toes up, as if sliding into base. She remembered. *Thank you, Lord.* He widened his stance and matched her position. Two feet from the ground, Victoria let out a scream. She continued to scream as they slid on mercifully soft soil. Jeff pulled down hard on the toggles in front of him to halt their speed. They were approaching another row of trees fast.

Jeff released a primal yell as he dug his heels in to the ground. His arms stung from the exertion of pulling on the toggles. They jerked to a stop ten feet away from a mean-looking group of apple trees.

Jeff lifted his head up to the heavens and sucked in a deep breath. His muscles, spent from the effort of swinging them to safety, lost their strength. He fell backward into the soil. Unfortunately, that meant Victoria fell back with him, against his burning lungs.

She turned slightly toward him. "Jeff? Jeff? Are you okay?"

"Yeah," he croaked. He fumbled with the clips until he could disconnect her harness from his. She rolled over onto the ground. On all fours, she took deep, shuddering breaths. He could hear her crawl toward his face. He closed his eyes, physically spent and mentally shaken from what had almost happened.

She placed a hand on his chest. "You saved us," she whispered and kissed his forehead. "You saved us."

He tried to ignore the surge of heat that rushed from his head to his toes from her kiss. "You're welcome." He looked up to find her face hovering over his, her helmet discarded, her dark hair surrounded by a halo of sunlight.

She pursed her lips. "Is anything broken?"

"No, I don't think so."

"So, you're sure you're all right? You don't need medical attention?"

"No, I'm fine. Just wiped out."

Her hand flung backward and slapped his shoulder hard. "What! Was! That!" She hit him again on his shoulder and leaned back on to her heels, her finger pointing at him. "You said it was safe! You said it'd be a breeze!" She gasped, and her eyes widened. "You spouted *numbers* to me!"

Jeff groaned. He should've never quoted statistics to an accountant. The adrenaline surged back into Jeff as he rolled away from her attack and sat up on his elbows. "Okay, okay! You're right! I said all those things! Victoria, it usually is safe. It's my fault. I thought I knew this land like the back of my hand."

She squinted and pursed her lips. "And?"

"And I should've double-checked or talked to my uncle. I didn't know he'd gotten into the tree business. Or, I calculated wrong. I guess it's possible we're on someone else's property." Jeff launched to his feet. "What about you? Are you okay?"

"Besides being scared to death, you mean? I'm simultaneously furious and indebted to you for my life." She crossed her arms and looked ahead at the budding trees. "It's very conflicting!"

"Your fists seem fine."

She didn't move but she raised one eyebrow and gave

him a side-glance. It could've been his imagination, but he thought he saw the faintest of grins.

"Victoria, I really am sorry." His neck took on the pain of his embarrassment and grew hot and prickly. He specifically hadn't taken much time to plan because he didn't want Drake to know where they were dropped. He'd had him file a flight plan to Payette and hadn't told him any more. He didn't want to risk Drake getting into trouble with cops or whoever was trying to kill them.

She leaned down and stroked the grass around her. "I will never take you for granted again."

"Are you talking to me or the ground?"

She glanced at him, her mouth forming a cute smirk. "What do you think?"

"Right." Jeff tilted his head to the left and then the right in an attempt to ease some of the stiffness. "Well, you have to admit no one could've followed us," he said, with a laugh.

She held up her index finger. "Too soon to joke about it, Jeff."

He cleared his throat. "Understood. Well, we better get started. We have a little hike to the truck." He gauged his surroundings for a moment. "If I can figure out where we are, that is." He unhooked his harness and let it drop to the ground, unzipped his jumpsuit down to his waist and pulled out his smartphone. "My GPS should make sure I don't lead us astray."

Victoria attempted to remove her own harness but let out an exasperated growl when it wouldn't budge.

"Let me get that." He loosened the straps on her right shoulder. "As you just experienced, there was a reason we make these harnesses so tight." He sensed her stare while he worked, and when he met her eyes an unfamiliar longing hit him in the chest. She was staring at his lips. "Thank you," she said, her voice so soft it made him weak in the knees.

He stepped backward. "That should do it."

"Thanks," she said softly.

She turned around and began unzipping the jump-suit. He stepped out of his own and began rolling it up, burrito-style. Without his strict routines and rules, without the cubicles and piles of work in his way, he was having the hardest time keeping his attraction to Victoria at bay. What horrible timing, too.

Victoria joined him, packing like a pro. She held her rolled-up jumpsuit under her arm and the diving harness like a one-handled backpack over her shoulder. The helmet and goggles dangled from her wrist. "What can I do to help?"

He handed her his smartphone. "It's trying to find our location. I need another minute," he said, folding the chute and placing the lines in an order he'd memorized years ago. "I don't want you thinking that what just happened is commonplace."

"Why? You afraid I won't go skydiving again?" She barked a laugh. "I think you should be more worried about your own safety from now on."

Jeff abruptly stopped and turned to look at her face. "Wasn't there even a second that you loved it?"

Victoria's cheeks reddened, and she moved her attention to the goggles on her wrist. "Before the close tree encounter, it was a pretty amazing experience. I had always wondered what it'd feel like to fly."

"Having to kick your legs up isn't normal."

"I figured that out for myself, thank you."

He squinted and in the distance could see a white pickup truck pulling into a gravel driveway a few acres away.

She looked up and visibly relaxed. "A stranger willing to help?"

Jeff's jaw clenched, and he stood, shifting his weight to accommodate for his gear.

"Who is it?"

"I don't know. Best case scenario, it's a hired hand. But, it's a small town, Victoria. That's the problem with small towns, it's easy to remember a face." He stomped a couple of steps to shake the loose dirt off his shoes. "Let's slip into the cover of the trees and get going before he spots us."

She handed him the phone, and he got his bearings. He led the way east in between a row of apple trees. The branches were low, but the rows were spread out enough they could walk side by side without getting a branch to the head.

Jeff sighed. "This might be a good time for me to give you a heads-up on my aunt and uncle, so you're prepared."

"That doesn't sound reassuring."

"They basically raised me." He glanced quickly at her, noting the gold-and-red flecks in her hair as the sunlight filtered through the tree branches. "But my uncle, well, he's a pretty regular guy, as farmers go, at least. My aunt and him are very simple in how they live. Think bare minimum without much technology or conveniences."

Victoria kept her eyes forward. "Like homesteaders? There's a real movement in that direction. Believe me, I've seen the blogs."

"They were doing this before any trend."

"So, they're trendsetters."

Jeff laughed. "Good one."

Victoria remained expressionless for a moment. "Except, why do I need to be prepared?"

"Her house is on the simple side."

"You mentioned that." She smiled tentatively. "I can handle simple."

He tilted his head from side to side. "Real simple."

"Electricity?"

Jeff scratched his head. "Yes, but minimal usage at all times. Uncle Dean wouldn't have it any other way. They haven't graduated to cell phones, but they do have a landline. No internet."

"Wow. Okay. Were your parents…did they live around here, too?"

Jeff slowed his gait. He didn't want to get into personal details. Coming here, telling her all about his uncle…he supposed it naturally led to such a discussion.

Victoria reached a hand in his direction and closed her eyes. "I'm sorry. I didn't mean to get too personal. Forget I asked."

He couldn't help but smile. Victoria had a way about her…she was always empathetic and compassionate. Even in team meetings, he could tell she was thinking about other people's feelings by the way she asked little update questions. Who had ever done that in his life? Taken that much interest?

In fact, Victoria seemed to know about everyone's lives in the department except for him. When he'd tried to talk to her in the past, she'd never made eye contact or engaged in any conversation. She had kept her answers to a minimum or a simple yes or no when he'd asked her how she was doing. Why?

He sighed. "I don't mind you asking. Yes, my parents

were originally from this area, but they didn't do as well. They left, for some reason. I don't know much about my father except he was considered a bad seed." He shook his head, as if the action would shake the thoughts away. "My mom raised me on her own for a while and then... brought me to my uncle. He's never told me why, and I never saw her again." Jeff blinked at the unexpected surge of emotion. Had he ever told anyone about his mom before? He couldn't recall ever being asked.

They walked in silence for a moment and stepped out of the protection of the trees. Ahead of them the portion of land without irrigation was dusty and dry, and the hill he remembered loomed above them, daunting. He pointed ahead at one of the many unofficial paths he remembered treading as a young man. "I hope you're up for a bit of a hike." He found her in deep concentration, as if she hadn't heard him. "Victoria?"

"How long has it been since you've visited?"

Jeff pursed his lips. "Too long."

He could feel Victoria staring at him. "And what do they think we're doing, then? They do know we're coming, don't they?"

At his silence her mouth fell. "Jeff! You didn't tell them we're coming? How'd you get arrangements for a car to be left?"

"No, no, I called. They just think we're, uh...coming for a visit."

She stepped closer to him, her pack bumping into his, and lowered her voice. "Who do they think I am?"

"I didn't tell them your name."

She stopped walking and crossed her arms. He turned around and held his arms out. "What?"

"You know what I meant."

"I said I was bringing a friend. A female friend."

"Did you tell them it was *just* a friend?"

Jeff blew out a long breath. "I didn't see the need to go into details."

"I see," she finally said.

"I know it's awkward," Jeff continued, "but they won't have any expectations."

She slapped her left hand on her leg and laughed. "You're kidding, right? Why do they think you're bringing me to visit other than for the chance to introduce me to the family? To check me out and see if I'm good enough for you?"

Jeff frowned. "They're not like that."

She closed her eyes and held up a finger. "Let me get this straight. You live about an hour away and you can't remember your last visit. So you don't even stay with them on the holidays, I'm guessing, either." She opened her eyes and sighed. "Jeff, give me one—just one—other reason why they could possibly think we're coming."

Jeff jutted his chin out. "Well." He inhaled deeply through his nose. "When you put it that way…"

Victoria groaned. "This is going to feel like a job interview for your hand in marriage." Instantly her cheeks flushed.

Jeff looked away, hoping she'd see it as a kind gesture to give her a moment to allow the embarrassment to fade, but truth be told, could she be right?

"Look, since I didn't have much time to plan this out, I think I've earned a little grace. This is the only place I could think of where we can stay without being traced or followed. Out here, we will be able to stay in ignorant bliss while we figure out a strategy to gather evidence. And, sure, I haven't visited them, but that doesn't mean they haven't met me in town. When I'm free, they drive up and meet me at a restaurant for birthdays and holidays."

She opened her mouth to respond, but her eyes darted past him. She pointed halfway up the hill. "I thought I saw those bushes move."

SEVEN

She watched Jeff furrow his brow. His skin slightly reddened from the wind, Jeff didn't look like a man to trifle with, and the way he was able to focus and get them out of a horrible situation earned her begrudging respect. "I'm sure it's nothing," he said. "I used to hike these hills all the time. Even if someone wanted to go and hide up there, they'd have to go through my uncle's land to get to it. Sagebrush and tumbleweed move easily without city buildings blocking the wind."

Victoria held on to her goggles with her right hand and used the left to shift the harness hanging from her shoulder. Her muscles ached, and all she wanted to do was rest. The sun hid behind a drifting cloud, reminding her there wasn't much left of the spring day. Early spring days in the mountains were short. Darkness returned before the workday was even done. She studied the terrain. How long had they been hiking? *What goes up must come down.* If they didn't hurry they wouldn't have enough sunlight to see every rock on the precarious trail that most likely zigzagged down the opposite side of the large hill.

Jeff held out his hand. "You up for this?"

She accepted his offering and held tight while she took a large step up and over the side of a boulder. "How long do you think this trail is?"

"Eh…not sure. It's not exactly a marked trail."

Victoria rolled her eyes.

"I saw that. But I suppose I deserve it," he finished. He stopped at the curve and peeked around a dead tree.

Victoria's lungs squeezed tight; she hoped they were just phantom pains. A reminder of an experience she wanted to forget. "Yes. Thank you. I'm sorry I'm not being gracious."

He shrugged and continued on the path, her hand still in his. "Don't apologize. I think you're amazing."

Victoria tried not to smile, but it was hopeless. Jeff stepped up onto a fallen log and pulled her up with him. He lifted her seemingly without any effort. In the office, his daily professional appearance showed no hints of such strength. She leaned back slightly, her balance off-kilter. She reached for his shoulders while he steadied her. Jeff looked into her eyes, and she turned away, suddenly dizzy.

"You okay?" Jeff asked, concern lacing his voice.

She inhaled sharply. "Yes. Just processing the day." It wasn't a lie.

He jumped down first, and she followed. She eyed the path they had just climbed. On both sides they were shielded by a collection of tumbleweed, tangled together into a large prickly wall. Jeff had been right about it being a location no one would notice. Not only were they seemingly in the middle of nowhere, the thorny desert growth kept them hidden. "Believe it or not, I used to love hiking."

"What changed?"

Victoria didn't know how to answer Jeff's question. What had changed? A memory of her parents' devastation after they'd lost everything in their company's stock scandal invaded her mind. They'd gone from being an average middle-class family to scrounging under couch cushions for every dime.

As a senior in high school, it was devastating to sell everything and leave her friends to move across country to live with her just-starting-out brother in Seattle. That was the moment she'd put aside her dream of a life of adventure, action and justice as an FBI agent. Instead she'd become a serious analyzer of risk and security. Her memory flashed to being asked to resign at her first job and her gut twisted, like it did every time she remembered the most humiliating day in her adult life.

"Life," she finally said. It was the simplest answer.

The daylight morphed into a purple haze. The sun's beautiful light show on the horizon wouldn't last much longer. She steeled herself against the exhaustion and began the hike back up the steep path. Her legs shook a little from the exertion. When this was all over, she promised herself she'd work out more often. Her lifestyle didn't prepare her for running away from fires and bombs, let alone skydives and hikes. Right now she just wanted a bubble bath. Did homesteaders use bubble bath?

Her favorite thing about hiking used to be the absence of talking. The only sounds were the crunching of her footsteps against the pebbles and the rustling of tumbleweed and sage as the wind slipped past. Jeff lent his strong hand to help her over another large boulder. It was so warm she let it go hesitantly, then stepped in front of him to take the lead. At least with him behind her, she wouldn't fear slipping as much.

She rounded the corner and saw a large sagebrush shake violently. "Jeff," she whispered, "do you think there are mountain lions in these parts?"

"Cougars? Sure, but I'm not too worried. They don't usually approach humans. There's enough wildlife around here to keep them busy."

Victoria nodded, but didn't take another step. She locked her sights on the thick stack of sage, tumbleweed and dead tree limbs. Maybe her eyes were playing tricks on her?

In her peripheral vision she saw a large animal jump out of the bush. She instinctively screamed, threw her hands up and took a step back, right into Jeff's arms. He was immovable and pressed his hands against the back of her shoulders to steady her. "Whoa. It's just a wild turkey." He laughed. "She's more scared of you than you are of her."

Victoria watched the large bundle of feathers flapping up the hill. "That…that huge thing was a wild turkey? But it didn't have a gobble, gobble! It was just a gigantic black bird thing."

"Trust me. It was a wild turkey hen." He stepped to her side, clearly about to resume the lead. "City girl," he said.

She clenched her jaw. How dare he tease her after the day she'd had? "Well, excuse me, mister, if I haven't seen a whole lot of wild turkeys in my—" Victoria stopped at the sight of Jeff's face. He turned pale and his eyes widened.

"Don't. Move. An. Inch." Jeff bit the words out. His eyes were wide as he looked at something behind her shoulder. Jeff squatted down slowly with his arm outstretched to the right side. "I think we just made a bobcat lose his turkey dinner. I'm grabbing this stick. Stay calm.

Bobcats don't usually attack humans, but we might've angered him."

Victoria couldn't help it. She trembled. If something was about to attack her, she wanted to see it approach and be on defense. She deliberately turned in a smooth, unhurried motion. A large, wild cat with a mixture of spots and stripes and shaggy hair crouched with one paw up in the air, no doubt ready to pounce.

"Go away!" Jeff yelled. He swung a jagged tree limb out in front of him. "Leave! Go!"

The cat didn't show any signs of leaving as Jeff stepped closer. He swung the limb in front of him, making a wide arc in front. The cat seemed to take offense at Jeff's movements. It released a growl of its own that took Victoria's breath away. So deep and with such vibration, it made her fear for her life. The cat's eyes were wide and focused on her now. She couldn't lose this staring contest.

Victoria kept one arm up in the air and stood on her tiptoes like all the survival guides she'd read instructed, but she slipped her other hand into the fanny pack. Jeff swung the stick again, and the bobcat switched his attention back to Jeff. She took advantage of the distraction and felt for the trigger button of the pepper spray. If she could just spray a little in the air, the cat should get enough of a whiff to run away before getting hit with it. In theory, she didn't need to actually shoot at the cat, unless it became absolutely necessary.

She wrapped her four fingers around the can and flicked her thumb over the safety switch. In one swift motion she yanked her hand out of her purse, turned her face sideways and sprayed pepper spray in the direction of the cat. It leaped a good six feet up, twisted in midair and bounded away. "Cover your face!" Victoria yelled, spun around and pulled her own shirt up enough to cover her eyes as she felt the wind shift at her back. The wind was taking the pepper spray with it.

Victoria sighed in relief, then turned to find a stunned Jeff. She couldn't resist. She twirled the can in her fingers and slid it back into her pocket like it was a gun holster. "Now, what were you saying about city girls?"

Jeff laughed. There certainly was a different side to the type-A kind accountant, and he liked it. His parched mouth distracted him. He wasn't a man accustomed to missing meals; in fact, his typical meal included a lot of protein, fruit and vegetables. His stomach growled loudly at the thought.

A twinge of empathy for the bobcat was replaced by an urgency to get Victoria to safety.

"Are you absolutely sure no one can connect you to your uncle's place? You didn't tell anyone? Not even on one of your dates?" The last word out of her mouth was said with such harsh emphasis he turned to face her.

She shook her head and put a hand over her eyes. "I don't know what got into me. I'm sorry, Jeff. I have no right to be jealous." Her eyes flashed open in horror, and her hand dropped to cover her mouth.

Jeff spun back to the trail and quickened his steps, lest she see the giant grin splayed across his face. "You're jealous?" He tried to make the smile diminish, but it was stubborn.

"That's…that's not what I meant to say." He heard her feet shuffling behind him, trying to catch up. "What I meant to say was…it isn't any of my business. Because why would I be jealous? I have no reason to be jealous.

Sleep deprivation makes me say weird things. I mean, honestly…"

Jeff laughed. She was protesting a little too much to be believable, but he had mercy on her. He turned around, both hands up. "Okay. Message received. And to answer your question, no, I haven't told anyone about this place except you."

Her eyes widened, and she nodded. They reached the top of the hill, and his chest puffed with a surge of pride. Below him was his uncle's farm. Mounds and rows had already been prepped for the seed that would no doubt be spread in the coming weeks. And while he couldn't see the house from this vantage point, he knew it was just past the group of trees used for windbreak.

A hundred feet to the north, he spotted the vehicle that had caused so much grief years ago. The old green pickup truck sat alone, but it didn't look unloved. The sun gleamed off its shiny coating.

"I've never seen an old truck look in such good condition aside from the occasional classic car show my brother and dad made me tag along to."

Despite Victoria's admiration, Jeff couldn't get past what the truck represented. He'd let his impatience get the best of him and made a bad decision to get what he wanted, the truck. And, even though he'd made amends a decade ago, a sting of disgrace accompanied every glance at the vehicle, which was why he'd never taken it with him. Instead, he paid the insurance and licensing and let his uncle use it as a farm truck. Clearly, his uncle kept it maintained.

He felt Victoria studying him. "What's wrong?"

"Nothing."

She took a deep breath. "I'm flying blind here, Jeff.

I'm grateful you made the plan to get us somewhere safe for the night because I needed someone to take the lead. And I know you're used to managing me as your supervisor, but—like you've pointed out—so far the plan isn't going as intended. So, how about we start communicating?" She crossed her arms over her chest. "I feel like you're keeping something from me."

"There's nothing you need to know," he said softly. "It's been a long day for me, too." He watched her face soften with compassion, and he was almost prompted to say more, but he'd already offered her too much of his past for one day. She walked by his side down the trail to the truck.

Jeff had never been so thankful to be back behind the wheel of a vehicle. Normally he lived for the outdoors and adventure, but today was too much for him. And if he inadvertently put Victoria in a position of danger again, he wouldn't be able to forgive himself.

She rubbed her eyes. "I'm so stiff and tired."

He watched her sink into the passenger seat and recalled her words. While he didn't want to share more of his past, he didn't want her to feel as if she was being managed either. "You were right, Victoria. I'm not good at sharing my plans. I'm pretty used to doing things solo, or at least leading whatever I'm doing. So here's the plan so far. I can't in good conscience let us stay with my aunt and uncle without telling them we're in danger."

She held up a hand. "I completely agree. If you have any reservations, we just leave. I'm so tired I think I can sleep anywhere."

He swallowed hard. He hadn't expected her to be so protective of them, as well.

He pressed the brake as they transitioned from the dirt road to a gravel road. "Prepare yourself."

While Jeff may have warned Victoria, he really needed to warn himself. He mentally did the math; it'd been three years since he'd visited home. While Uncle Dean owned a phone, neither held much value in reaching out and calling. Aunt Katie mailed him a handwritten letter the fifth of every month, like clockwork, but the letters had to do with the season changes on the farm or the happenings at church. She never mentioned anything personal and never asked him any questions either.

Victoria flipped open the visor and groaned. She rapidly wiped at her cheeks, then unleashed her hair and began finger combing it.

"Victoria, I'm sorry. You misunderstood. I didn't mean you needed to prepare yourself that way…you look beau—you look fine, just the way you are."

She dropped her hands and blinked slowly, as if trying to figure him out. He decelerated at the sight of the house a block ahead, the gravel crunching underneath the tires. Surprisingly, it was a sound that still brought him comfort and left him with the desire to walk through harvested fields. When he passed the barn, Victoria gasped and leaned forward. "I'm so glad it's not dark yet or we would've missed this."

Ah. He'd forgotten the beauty. Could there be a woman alive who wouldn't appreciate the rows and rainbows of colorful flower beds adorning the edges of the house? If national landscapers were placed in a competition against his aunt, it'd be a close race. "They're pretty," he acknowledged, "but I can't share your enthusiasm. I spent way too many a day working in those beds. My job was to plant and weed all summer long. They're lots of work."

She eyed him. "I thought you said you hadn't been here in years?"

"Who do you think had to dig and plant these beds that have been blooming all those years?"

"Well, they're gorgeous."

He nodded. "Aunt Katie's gifted. I imagine if she wanted, she could make a decent wage in Boise." He shifted the car into Park and stepped out.

"Jeffrey."

He looked up to find his aunt walking quickly down the porch steps. Her hands squeezed together in front of her body, and she beamed at him. It was the same position she'd used every afternoon after school, waiting for him to walk home using shortcuts across the property. Even though he stood almost a foot above her, he almost expected her to hold a hand out to inspect his backpack for any homework.

Jeff approached, and she patted a firm hand on his back. "So, where is she?" she looked up at him, her gray, shoulder-length hair waving loose in the wind. "You didn't leave her in the car, did you?"

Jeff's shoulders sagged. "Aunt Katie, you didn't give me a chance."

She waved a slightly bent finger at him. "Don't sass me, Jeffrey," she teased.

He jogged back to open Victoria's door and found her batting against her shirt. "I'm probably covered in dog hair and dirt. Just a sec," she muttered.

He looked over his shoulder to find Katie with her hands on her hips. "Uh-oh," he told Victoria. "You're making me look ungentlemanly."

"Is that a word?" Victoria laughed, then accepted his outstretched hand. "I was trying to look presentable."

He placed his palm on her back as he walked her over to Katie, who by then had gone back up the stairs to the porch. Aunt Katie poked her head inside the house and hollered for Uncle Dean as they approached.

"You must be Katie," Victoria said. She held out her hand. "Jeff has told me so much about you."

Aunt Katie accepted Victoria's hand and covered it with her other hand. It was the closest thing Aunt Katie came to an embrace. "Well, he did? Then I'll be glad to set you straight." A giant smile splayed across her face.

Jeff watched as his adoptive mother slipped her arm into Victoria's and began walking her the length of the wraparound porch, giving her a tour of the property. He shook his head and kicked his toe at a knot in the porch. Victoria was right. Aunt Katie thought he had brought his future bride home.

Victoria was pretty—beautiful, even—and he enjoyed her company more than any dinner date. He thought the signs of attraction were mutual, but she also avoided eye contact like the plague, which usually meant a lack of interest, pure and simple. Jeff kicked a pebble off the porch. Now wasn't the time to be thinking about a future bride anyway.

While Aunt Katie waxed eloquently about the beauty of the land around them, Jeff followed silently. His phone vibrated. The text was from April: Police just asked if any of us know where you are. Everyone says your car blew up. Where are you?

EIGHT

Jeff's eyes narrowed. A second later there was a similar text from the supervisor in marketing. If Victoria's phone hadn't already been dinging, he imagined it would soon. He held the button and turned his phone off. "Victoria, I don't have a cell phone charger," he interjected over Katie's tour. "Maybe you should turn your phone off and save battery for tomorrow."

He could see the exhaustion on her face as she turned. Her eyes barely widened and her smile faded. "Oh. That's a good idea. I took off my fanny pack in the truck. I'll go grab it."

"Allow me." Jeff turned and strode to the truck before she could change her mind. He looked over his shoulder and saw her shoulders droop as she leaned on the deck's railing and continued to listen to Aunt Katie. Victoria had had next to no sleep the previous night, and the toil of today's events looked to be catching up fast.

He focused on the truck with a decisive nod. It was true they needed to conserve battery power, but he also wanted the phones off, and the batteries removed, so there would be no chance of anyone tracing them. He in-advertently spotted three texts on the home screen of her phone. Two female names he didn't recognize had asked about the fire, and one male, Nate, wanted to check in. Who was Nate—a friend or a boyfriend? A surge of curiosity tempted him to read more, but just as his finger reached for the power button the phone vibrated.

Think you can run away? Thought you were smarter than that. Return to office unless you'd like more of your life destroyed.

Jeff's heart raced. He glanced at the sender. It was a series of random letters, presumably sent from a texting app, which meant it'd be virtually untraceable. If Victoria had any more worry placed on her shoulders, she was sure to fall apart. He might not have been able to stop the horrible things from happening, but the least he could do was protect her. Besides, the office reference had to be bait for a trap. He quickly accessed her settings, turned off location services, removed the battery and stored the phone.

He leaned against the truck. If he told Victoria now, she'd never sleep. For tonight, he'd keep the texts to himself so Victoria could rest while he stayed on guard. That is, if his aunt and uncle would have them. He noticed Victoria's wallet and a small case inside the fanny pack. As her only possessions, she probably would want to have those tonight, but he purposefully left their phones in the truck's glove compartment.

He reached the porch and found Victoria missing.

Aunt Katie came around the corner holding a bundle of fresh herbs. "Don't worry. She asked to freshen up, so I sent her on in. She looks exhausted, Jeffrey."

Jeff hung his head. He wanted to wait until he saw

Uncle Dean to explain the situation, but it didn't seem prudent to waste any more time. "Aunt Katie, we're not here for fun. In fact, we might not be able to stay at all. Victoria's in danger, and while I think no one has followed us, there is the small potential of putting you in harm's way."

Uncle Dean's voice resonated behind him. "Sounds to me like you've come to the right place, then."

Jeff spun around and searched his uncle's face for any signs of disapproval or mistrust. "You don't even know the situation yet."

Uncle Dean straightened. "Seems like you wouldn't have come here if you didn't think this was your safest option." His stern face shifted into a giant smile. "We see you so rarely, we'll take you when we can get you. Your aunt would kill me if I sent you away now." He chuckled at himself.

Aunt Katie rested a hand on his arm. "So, you're not here to introduce us to your future—"

"No, I'm afraid not."

Aunt Katie put her other hand on her chest. "You could've warned me. I babbled on and on about—"

"Yeah, well, I may have been a little preoccupied at the time I called." He held up his hands. "Victoria already took me to task on that."

She gave a satisfied smile. "So, she's good for you, then." Katie patted his arm. "You thought right to come here. I hope you're hungry. I planned a big dinner, and I don't expect to eat it all myself."

"Yes, ma'am," he said, reflecting on how much of a softie his aunt had become in the years he'd been away. He inhaled deeply, searching for signs of Aunt Katie's cooking. As if on cue, his stomach let out a small roar.

"I'll get supper on," Katie said. She took Jeff's elbow and walked alongside him and Uncle Dean into the house. "Tell us, why is she in danger?"

She washed the dirt off her hands, scrubbing hard, hoping the pain would keep her from crying. If she started crying now, she wouldn't be able to stop. And she couldn't even freshen up her lip balm or mascara because those were left in her cosmetic case.

Victoria stomped her foot. Anger was good. It'd keep her away from despair. No home. No job. And possibly jail in her future. They had to find evidence.

She heard the back door open and close a few times, so she hustled back outside. She spotted Jeff in the distance, near a pond, hollering.

Her bones and muscles were overused and weary after the long day as she walked the dirt path. She joined Jeff in the long grasses next to the pond. "What are you doing?"

"Helping Aunt Katie by gathering the chickens before dinner. You didn't see her in the house? She must be getting you some clothes."

"You told her?" She couldn't hide her surprise.

"I was vague, but I did tell them you were in danger. They don't know we're being framed. The less they know, the safer they will be. Uncle Dean opened the gun cabinet for fast access, but the only way to the house is the half-a-mile gravel driveway in front of the house. Gravel works like an alarm system. We'll hear them before we see them."

"What about the path we drove on earlier?"

"It ends at the irrigation canals, which are full and run parallel to the edge of the property for miles. There's no way over those canals without risk of death. You're safe tonight, Victoria."

She tried to ignore the way her heart pounded when he said her name. Her hair blew backward in the wind, as she stared at the small ripples moving across the water. "I keep wondering what we're supposed to do. My mind refuses to slow down, even while I'm praying for wisdom."

They stood shoulder to shoulder staring ahead. "You need to be able to rest, Victoria. We don't know what's ahead, but worrying won't help you now."

"I know I should stop worrying but it's easier said than done. If only I knew our next step."

He sighed. "I actually had an idea. Mr. Wagner lives about forty-five minutes southeast of here."

She spun toward him. "What? Why would he live so far from work?"

"He has a condo in the city, but he has an amazing house in the foothills that looks down over the valley. Haven't you ever noticed the line of houses twinkling in the night? That's where the elite live."

"How does the head of the marketing department become part of the so-called elite? And how would he swing that kind of mortgage?"

"He invited me and the rest of the supervisors for a holiday get-together. He made some joke about inheritances not being all they're cracked up to be. I got the impression it was his wife who had the inheritance, though."

"You don't actually trust him, do you? Because in my mind he's the number-one suspect!"

"No, I don't trust him anymore, but we need answers sooner than later, and I don't know a better place to start. I thought about calling him, but tomorrow is Saturday, and there's no guarantee he would pick up. I don't want to raise any alerts. Besides, I want to see his face, see his eyes, when I confront him."

Victoria shuddered. "I don't see how he could be innocent."

"I understand why you would think that, but from my point of view, before all of this happened, he was a man I respected. I need to talk to him."

"When do we go?"

"Oh, you're not going with me." He threw a thumb over his shoulder. "You'll be safe here. If Wagner does happen to be behind any of this, I want you out of danger."

She pursed her lips but didn't reply for a moment. "Tonight?"

"No, I think we could both do with a rest."

The wind picked up, and she rubbed her hands over her arms for extra warmth.

"You're cold." He began unbuttoning his flannel shirt, revealing a white shirt underneath.

She shook her head violently. "No, that's sweet, but I think I'm just nervous," she said, teeth chattering. "I'm… I'm not a rule breaker. This feels like I'm diving off a cliff."

He put a hand on her shoulder. "You already dove off a plane today and survived. This is hard, but we'll get through it."

"But how?" She took a small step back, her eyes wide. "I'm a type-A person. I need to control things, and everything is spinning—you already know I'm horrible about not worrying." A gust of wind blew her hair across her face. She was almost thankful for the sudden veil to hide her emotions.

"We're in this together." He brushed his hand across

her jawline and against the side of her neck, pushing her hair away from her face. His gaze drifted to her lips.

She blinked and opened her mouth in surprise. Jeff jerked and pulled back, as if he hadn't known what he was doing. "Thank you for the encouragement," she whispered, then turned and marched back to the house.

Victoria's fingers drifted to her lips. She looked over her shoulder and found him watching her. Despite her best efforts, she smiled, and immediately turned away.

What if he had kissed her? Her heart sped up. And while he'd put an end to it before it even began, his gesture had shocked her out of her worry, made her feel secure and protected. Even if it was a delusion, it was a welcome one. And yet, she couldn't let him think she wanted more than a friendship. He might deny having fear of commitment, but until he explained himself, with evidence, she'd trust her instincts.

She approached the house, alone with her thoughts and prayers, and allowed the smell of grass and lavender to soothe her along the way. The moment Jeff mentioned that name, Wagner, she knew she wasn't going to agree to his plan. She also guessed that if she argued with him, he'd just leave without telling her, and there was no way she'd let him get away with that. No more letting him lead the way. She was the one who'd found the conspiracy in the first place, so she should be the one to find the persons responsible for framing them. She just needed to come up with her own plan before morning.

On the porch steps, she found herself face-to-face with a man who didn't look all that different from Jeff, just much older. He wore a red-and-blue plaid shirt, jeans and hiking boots. With silver hair, dark eyes and a grin that held both mischief and welcome, he held out his right hand. "You must be Vicky."

"Victoria," she corrected, with a nod.

He opened the back screen door. "Welcome. I hope you're hungry."

An assault of smells hit Victoria: freshly baked bread, onions and butter, garlic, and…marshmallows? Her stomach and mouth eagerly waited to find out. She stepped inside the all-wooden kitchen and dining room. Moments ago, she'd rushed in and out so fast she hadn't taken time to appreciate her surroundings. Gorgeous craftsmanship greeted her at every turn. The gleaming shine of the oak floors stopped her in her tracks. She admired the woven rug of reds and yellows at the back door.

Katie watched her, a pot holder and a large serving bowl in one hand and a wooden spoon in the other. Her eyebrows rose, then she looked away with a smile and went back to serving without another word. Dean pulled back a chair for Victoria. She'd only seen men open doors and pull out chairs for women in movies. Never had anyone given her that grace besides employees paid to open doors at restaurants. "Thank you." So this was why Jeff always opened doors and focused on being a gentleman.

A few moments later, Jeff walked in, slightly flushed. "Chickens are all taken care of, Aunt Katie. Food smells delicious."

Jeff took a seat next to the freshly baked loaf of bread Katie had just placed on the table. Either from embarrassment or hunger or both, Jeff only had eyes for the food on the table. Katie served him a large helping of chicken potpie. Victoria watched as thick gravy slowly descended out of the crust onto the plate with carrots swimming along for the ride. The stress on Jeff's face immediately vanished and was replaced with a grin.

Dean bowed his head. Jeff and Katie followed suit. Victoria wasn't used to the absence of conversation, but she took the moment to silently pray for their situation.

She wanted nothing more but to change into her lounge pants and head for bed. Once her hunger was satisfied, her eyelids grew heavy along with her limbs. She played the part of the good guest, though, and helped Katie wash the dishes. If only Jeff's aunt and uncle believed in dishwashers. It seemed like the longest day of her life.

Jeff nodded to the back door. "I need to show you something. It won't take long."

NINE

Jeff stepped outside and inhaled. There simply was no comparison to the city. The air was rich with the smell of flowers, grass and trees. As darkness settled on the valley, the animals fell silent except for the occasional moo. Only the faint, far away sounds of crickets harmonizing drifted through the night.

Victoria followed him to the east side of the house. Just as he'd remembered, three wooden Adirondack chairs sat on the wraparound deck.

"I thought a little stargazing might help you relax and get some sleep tonight. We both need to unwind. Uncle Dean is watching the driveway."

"That was thoughtful."

"It's been known to happen." He shook his head. "Although with you, it seems to come more naturally."

She either didn't hear him or didn't want to acknowledge what he'd said. Taking her seat, she looked up. "Gorgeous," she whispered.

"You won't see stars like this in town. The city lights keep you from seeing their brightness."

"Do you miss it?"

He turned to find her bright, sapphire-colored eyes

staring at him. "The stars? Sometimes, I suppose, but not consciously."

"No, living out here. Them." She jerked her thumb back toward the house.

He shrugged. "They weren't always like this. Uncle Dean is still quick to shut me down for asking questions. It's difficult to have a real conversation."

"They were strict guardians," she guessed.

"That would be an understatement."

"How so?"

He rubbed his forehead with unease. He became talkative when he was tired. His eyes swept over the skies, and he pointed to the right. "I can't be certain, but I think that's Saturn hanging low in the horizon."

She didn't take the bait. "How old were you when your mom brought you here?"

"Six."

Victoria placed a hand on her heart. "That must have been tough."

"Sure, but at least they took me in. I'm very thankful they didn't let me bounce around the foster care system." He pointed to the left. "The Big Dipper is my favorite."

This time it worked. "It's my favorite, too. Probably because it's the only one I can consistently recognize." Victoria stretched, yawned and released a contented sigh.

He smiled. The fresh air and quiet had the desired effect on her. Finally, something had gone right. He was still embarrassed by his gesture at the pond. Why had he let himself reach out to her? Now she'd think of him differently, as the guy who'd almost kissed her. He blamed the near-death experiences, but Jeff still wanted to explain himself. He opened his mouth to quip that at least her shivering had stopped but closed it just as quickly.

They sat in a companionable silence staring at the sparkling view for almost half an hour. A warm sleepy feeling passed over him. He glanced at Victoria and, to his surprise, found her eyes closed.

Standing up, he gently touched her shoulder. "Victoria," he whispered. She didn't budge. He grabbed the back of the chair and rocked it back and forth. "Victoria," he said, a little louder. Her mouth fell open slightly.

He rubbed his hands on the front of his pants to warm them after sitting idle in the chilly air. Well, this certainly was a predicament. He couldn't leave her out alone in the dark all night. He tried in vain once more to gently rouse her.

Not so much as a flinch. He wanted her to relax enough so she could sleep, he just hadn't expected it to work so fast.

Squatting, he slipped his hand underneath and through the space between the back of her neck and hair until his elbow cradled her head. His other hand slipped underneath her knees. Thankfully, he was helped in his mission by the form of the Adirondack chair. On a silent count of three, he lifted and brought her form up against his chest.

He looked down at her relaxed face. She was gentle and peaceful, so beautiful. Turning, he took a step toward the house. Faint yips and howls from the coyotes in the hills reached his ears. Victoria's right hand and head simultaneously jerked up, the palm of her hand hitting his chin.

"Ouch." He stumbled back a few steps and almost lost his grip but stayed the course.

Her eyes red, she looked around wildly until her gaze met his. She stared at him, startled, wordless and clearly confused.

"You were asleep."

She tried to sit up in his arms. He lowered his left arm so she could fully stand. "Can you manage?"

She nodded, blinking rapidly, her hand resting against his chest. "Sorry." Her voice was raspy from deep sleep. "So tired."

"This way," he whispered, and guided her the rest of the way into the house. The lone light in the kitchen woke her fully.

"I'm so embarrassed," she said, yawning.

"No need." He pointed down the hallway. "Your room is to the right. I'll be on the couch, keeping watch."

"Thanks," she mumbled. "Jeff, why don't you visit more? It's such a lovely place."

He smiled. "We can talk more tomorrow. Get some sleep."

Her heavy eyelids seemed to agree, and she shuffled to the guest room door. Jeff's gut twisted. He knew if he told her the reason, she'd have to wait a long time for sleep to come. But in his mind, the answer came quickly. Here, he was still the guy no one could trust—the guy Uncle Dean couldn't trust.

The sun refused to be ignored. Victoria pulled the covers over her face. She wanted to enjoy every minute underneath the thick quilt. She remembered what it had been like being held by Jeff, cradled in his arms. She'd been safe, and he'd smelled so good...

Her eyes flew open. It would be best to forget the sensation of him holding her. The sunshine bounced off the white walls and the shined wooden floors. She sat up in the full-size bed and smelled something clearly containing bacon and onions. Her stomach growled in agreement, and the clock told her that it was almost seven.

Stepping on the cold floor, she slipped on the socks, jeans and navy button-down shirt Katie had left on the top of the dresser. She crossed the hallway to brush her teeth. The memories of waking up to fire, watching Jeff's car blow up and finding embezzled money in her account all hit her at once. If only she could go back to bed and pretend it never happened.

She opened the bathroom door and followed her nose. To her surprise, Aunt Katie sat on the living room couch wearing a thick terry cloth robe. Katie smiled, her head down reading a Bible that lay on her lap. "Good morning." She closed her eyes for a moment.

Victoria looked around, unsure of what to do. While Aunt Katie had a very soft voice, her formal manner intimidated Victoria.

Katie's eyes flashed open. "You have a few minutes before breakfast is ready."

"Where is Jeffrey?" Victoria asked, feeling only slightly guilty that she referred to him by his full name. He may not approve, but when in Rome...

"I'm not sure. I thought he was feeding the animals with Dean, but Dean returned a while ago. It's possible he's visiting his favorite spot."

Victoria crossed the room to sit in the rocking chair. "His favorite spot?"

Katie looked her up and down, assessing her. "Ever since he was six he loved to sit underneath the willow tree. Dean once told him it was his mother's favorite spot when she was younger, and I think it's his way of having something in common with his mom."

She looked out the window. The green truck was gone.

Victoria frowned. What if Jeff had taken the truck so he could sneak off to Wagner's without her? "Is the willow tree far from here?"

"It's just past the barn, about a quarter mile down the hill at the edge of the property. If you start seeing cows, you've gone too far."

She bolted out the door before Katie could say another word and jogged down the path toward the barn. She was supposed to beat him to the punch with a new plan, but instead she'd gone and slept the night away. If he decided to play hero and leave her here without a phone or transportation, she was going to kill him.

Three minutes later, her side hurt, but she reached the side of the barn. She slowed to a walk to catch her breath. A couple hundred feet beyond, the green truck sat next to a group of trees, and just past it, stood Jeff. He wasn't underneath the willow tree but right next to it facing the shimmering pond. Bordering the water, rows of tall prairie grass swayed with the breeze. His hands were behind his back and his head was down.

She approached slowly and quietly. Even though he hadn't left yet, she wanted to make sure he couldn't go to see Wagner without her. The closer she stepped, the more she strained her eyes. Fifty feet to the east of the willow tree was a burial plot. One small headstone came into focus. Clearly homemade, the stone was marked Scarecrow, Best Dog Ever.

Victoria took another step, and a twig snapped. Jeff swung around, his eyes wide. "Did something happen? Are you okay?"

Her face heated. His words replayed in her memory. *I just prefer to not get attached in the first place.* And when she'd suggested he had a fear of commitment, he'd said, *I don't expect you to understand, Victoria, but it couldn't be farther from the truth.* Was it possible she'd misjudged him? Was it more a fear of losing the ones he loved?

"Victoria?"

"I—I was worried. I didn't know where you were," she stammered.

He surprised her with a grin. "I'm at your service."

"Breakfast is ready."

He nodded and strode to the truck. "Hop in."

Following his lead, Victoria remained quiet until they found his aunt and uncle in the kitchen sipping cups of coffee.

Aunt Katie raised an eyebrow but said nothing about Victoria's odd behavior moments ago. "Do you like coffee?"

"Adore it," she responded.

She examined Jeff's face. His eyes were slightly glassy, but he was smiling. "Did you sleep at all?"

"Uncle Dean gave me a turn to sleep."

Uncle Dean nodded at Victoria and walked out of the kitchen, his head down, a sly grin on his face. Jeff accepted the French press from his aunt and filled a cup of coffee for her. "I basically passed out."

She accepted the cup and looked at the dark liquid. "Do you have creamer?"

"Why say you like coffee if you're just going to water it down?" Katie asked, with a laugh.

Jeff rolled his eyes. "She's teasing, Victoria. I can give you better than creamer. I can give you the real thing fresh from the source." He pulled at the fridge handle. Inside was a glass bottle, filled with smooth, succulent cream.

Victoria closed her eyes at her first sip. "You can't get this at the grocery store," she finally said.

Jeff laughed, watching her. "That's right."

They sat down at the long table and served themselves heaping helpings of a bacon, egg, hash-brown and onion casserole. "If I keep eating this way, I won't be able to fit into my clothes."

"Don't let her hear that." Jeff took a second helping. "Aunt Katie will have you doing the homesteaders' workout of sweeping, laundry, milking and feeding the chickens."

Jeff excused himself, which left Katie and Victoria to clean up, once again. Only the second meal she'd experienced, and Victoria already disliked the routine. "Don't you ever resent the men scattering when it's time to clean and clear?"

Katie scrubbed the casserole dish in the sink. "I suppose if he was lazy, yes. But I rested while Dean worked outside this morning." She looked out the kitchen window as her hands methodically circled around the dish. "When I grew up a farmer's daughter, I hated everything about it, but now I have the freedom to choose my role." She turned to Victoria, her eyes bright. "Freedom changes everything. I haven't always done it, but now when I wake up, I remind myself that I have the freedom to choose. I'm at peace with cleaning the dishes each day, because that's the job that I chose." She looked behind her, with a twinkle in her eye. "Dean wouldn't want it broadcasted, but he helps me dry dishes every night when company isn't here."

Victoria couldn't pin down exactly why, but her heart prickled.

Katie continued to talk while her hands swished in the

bubbles. "In the end, I get my value from Jesus. I walk with Him, I talk with Him and I enjoy the freedom and blessings and wisdom He gives me each day. And Jeffrey, that boy is such a blessing. Seeing him spread his wings and succeed in the city gives Dean and me new courage to spread our own wings." She looked out ◆ the window and smiled.

Victoria focused on her drying duties, wishing the awkwardness away. Why couldn't she do what Katie did? Why couldn't she be satisfied with her day-to-day life? Maybe if she'd had that peace, she'd never have gotten herself and Jeff into such an utter mess; maybe their futures wouldn't be hanging in the balance.

From the doorway, Jeff asked, "Aunt Katie, can I borrow Victoria for a moment?"

Katie nodded, still focused on the sink in front of her. Draping the towel flat on the countertop, Victoria followed Jeff outside. "Jeff, this has been nice, but time is slipping away. The longer we wait to gather evidence, the more likely it is we'll end up in jail."

He looked out into the pasture where four cows meandered around the uncut grass. "Not on my watch."

She'd never thought cows could look happy, but the light brown ones managed to embody that attitude. "So, what do you have in mind? Because I really don't think going to Wagner is wise. We need to come up with some other ideas before taking drastic measures."

"There's something I have to tell you. We received a threat."

TEN

She took the news better than expected, confirming his choice to let her sleep. "Where's my phone?" she asked. "We should check it to see if there are others." Her head tilted. "The police are asking questions...so that's why you want to go to Wagner? Maybe we should just go back to the office instead. Aren't you worried what they might do next?"

He nodded. "Yes, but we can't let a vague threat stop us now. We need to get answers fast."

She was making eye contact. Why would she avoid looking him in the eye for the past two years but now she would? Was that a sign of friendship? Suddenly he was glad she'd not made it a habit. When she turned her gorgeous eyes on him, all his protective walls shattered. "There may have been some truth to what you said yesterday."

"Oh?"

"April was the one who texted me about the police. Perhaps she wasn't okay with just being friends after all, but the feeling was not mutual."

Victoria simply pursed her lips. "That's really none of my business. When I thought about it, I realized I actually knew you better than I knew her," she said. "You and I may have never had any lengthy conversations but…"

"Actions mean more than words," he guessed.

She squared her shoulders. "So let's go," she said. "But we need to do this together."

He studied her a moment, then nodded. "Fine. I need to gather a few things and tell them we're leaving. I'd like you to take a couple changes of clothes, as well. Just in case."

He grabbed an old backpack from his closet and slipped in some clothes and a couple of old outfits Aunt Katie had set out in Victoria's room.

When he returned, Victoria was at the kitchen table, jotting down notes on a legal pad she'd found on Uncle Dean's desk. She was talking to herself, verbally recounting everything that had gone on that weekend. He never knew she—let alone any woman—could speak so fast.

"I'm hoping I'll see something new, some clue, some way to get us out of this mess." She tapped the table's shiny finish with her fingertips. "Are your aunt and uncle going to get annoyed if we leave and don't tell them where we're going or when to expect us back?"

"If they are, they won't tell me. They only get on my case if they feel like I'm sassing them. These past three years they've never once pressured me to come back home and visit."

"That must be nice," she said.

"You'd think." She aimed her confused stare at him, but he refused to acknowledge it.

Victoria resumed her furious writing. He set to work gathering a sack lunch. The one magnet on the refrigerator listed a verse from the book of Timothy: "For God hath not given us a spirit of fear; but of power, and of love, and of a sound mind."

Had his aunt and uncle ever feared anything? They never spoke as if they did. If they shared an opinion on something, which they rarely did, they did it with unwavering decisiveness. He couldn't imagine that Victoria feared much. Except, maybe, letting other people get hurt from something she could've prevented. His heart warmed at that passion.

Before the events of the weekend, Jeff personally thought he had become immune to fear. The way his heart sped up and his neck tightened every time he imagined Victoria hurt or both of them going to prison proved otherwise. The verse nagged at him. He spied Aunt Katie's Bible and picked it up. The next verse in Timothy revealed that the very person who wrote those words was already a prisoner. How could someone write encouragement like that when they were facing something so horrible themselves?

Aunt Katie's bookmark began to slip out. He caught it and tucked it back to her spot. 1 John. "There is no fear in love; but perfect love casteth out fear: because fear hath torment. He that feareth is not made perfect in love."

Jeff smirked. Whoever wrote that hadn't had someone they loved abandon them.

Victoria let out a loud sigh. Her black hair fell over her face. He could barely see her cute nose, her long eyelashes and her full mouth. He set back to his preparations.

"I feel like I'm missing something that's right in front of my face." Victoria sat up enough that he could see some of her writings now that her hair was out of the way.

At the top of the paper, "What We Know" was listed

on the left side and on the right side, "What We Don't Know."

Jeff almost laughed aloud. If ever there were a person more suited to being an accountant, they'd need to meet Victoria first to duke it out. She exemplified all things analytical and methodical with a large side of restrained passion. He could see the intensity in her eyes whenever she spoke. "What are you doing there?"

She looked up, flushed and tilted her head. "I asked God for wisdom, and my mind started racing. I figured it'd be disrespectful not to take notes."

He grinned. "Or it could be you've never had French press coffee before. Aunt Katie learned how to make coffee from the Amish."

"It was really strong, wasn't it?"

"Aunt Katie likes it to be strong enough to arm wrestle."

She propped up her elbow. "Well, I think I'm ready, then."

Jeff acted like he was taking her offer to arm wrestle, but instead pulled her to a standing position. She laughed then sighed. "It doesn't seem right to laugh when our lives are in danger."

"It does when you're living in the moment," Jeff answered.

He caught sight of the entire paper.

What We Know:
- Heads of departments had access to direct deposit
- Evidence on flash drive stolen
- Guy in ugly red ball cap is connected to company
- Someone blocked our company access
- I was right all along

Jeff slipped the pen out of her hand. He jotted down next to her first bullet: *Wagner. Me. Denise. April, Human Resources. Patrick, Marketing. Hunter, Operations.* He tapped the pen to the paper, making little dots as he tried to remember the rest of the department head names. Victoria frowned and grabbed the pen back from him. "We can go over this on the way."

Once in the truck, she turned to a new sheet of paper. "Help walk me through how we make the generators. The generator links up to solar panels that are installed at the same time, right? And, whenever the solar energy reaches a certain level, it powers the generator, which shuts off your electricity for the consumer, thereby saving them money on their electricity bill."

She wrote, *Bright Green Solar.* "CleanSpark was one company. I think they must've provided the spark plugs or something. They disappeared off the expense report. Jeff, correct me if I'm getting any of this wrong. Green Recoil made the recoil starter thing. EnviroGasket also comes to mind. I'm assuming they supplied the gaskets," Victoria said. She slapped her forehead. "I can't remember any more!"

Something nagged at the corner of his mind.

Jeff had started working in Earth Generator's assembly department in the factory warehouse after graduating high school. He had continued to work there while he completed his degree at the community college. It wasn't until he'd let some of the guys talk him into a Saturday skydive that he'd realized his dream to become a certified skydiving instructor. The first step had been to earn a bunch more money.

Thankfully, he'd talked with his supervisor, who'd put in a good word at the corporate offices. They hired from within before advertising publicly, which had worked in his favor. He'd found himself pushing forms in Human Resources. From there, it had been a slow but steady climb to a department supervisor.

He could see some of the assembly lines in his head but not specific parts. Didn't they put together their own gaskets? The names of the companies on Victoria's list... they sounded too...too perfect. He looked in the rearview mirror and stiffened.

Victoria spun in her seat to look out the rear window. "What is it?" She gasped.

"I know. I see it, too, but we don't know for sure if it's a red Range Rover. We are too far away to tell for certain. We need to stay calm. Besides, they don't know this truck."

"He's coming up too fast, don't you think?"

"That's what concerns me," Jeff admitted. "Turn around and act natural. We're going to take a sharp turn up ahead and see if he follows."

Victoria did as he asked and even sank deeper into her chair. Jeff veered onto a gravel road faster than he should have and fought to keep the steering wheel straight. There was a fork a mile down the road if he needed to lose whoever was behind them.

A couple minutes later, he sighed. "I think we're safe."

Victoria groaned. "No one's following us?"

"I don't think so, but I'll use the gravel roads to take us to Wagner's. It'll take us longer, but it might be the safer choice."

If energy could be measured, her tank was running on empty. The coffee jitters dissipated. She sagged against the armrest of the truck. No wonder petite Aunt Katie was able to get so much work done with that level of caffeine coursing through her veins. Jeff wore sunglasses and stayed focused on the highway in front of him, so she couldn't tell if he experienced the same sensation. Maybe he always made his coffee the Amish way.

Clusters of wild sunflowers peppered the hillside. It was amazing something so beautiful could grow wild in the desert.

What if this was the last free weekend she could experience the world? She felt the sting in her eyes and nose.

Jeff took another sharp left turn.

"There was no street sign. How do you know you're on the right street?"

He shrugged. "I grew up here. I know all the back roads, and believe me, there is no shortage. Used to be logging roads, I think. Now you won't see too many trees out here. We had more than our share of forest fires a few years back, and the rest of the area is either orchards or farmland."

"So, I think we should practice what you'll say to Wagner."

He raised an eyebrow. "I've worked with the man long enough that I think I'll know when I see him what to do."

She curled her upper lip. "You're kidding, right? You don't have a plan?" The truth was, if she had a better idea of what to do next, she'd be doing it.

The road took a sudden incline and curved around a large hill, then another.

"We're almost there. There's a street above Wagner's street. We'll go there first and do a little surveillance before popping in on him. We need to make sure there are no Range Rovers in the vicinity."

Each mile-long curve gradually increased their altitude. Twenty minutes later, they crested a giant hill. Jeff drove past the turn and onto another gravel road. A glance over her shoulder revealed a long line of impressive houses and manicured lawns.

She whistled. "You weren't kidding. These houses are amazing."

"I'm trying to put myself in Wagner's shoes for a second. If you had a sizeable inheritance, would you still work if you didn't need to?"

"If I weren't married or planning a family, maybe not. But if I were married with kids, I'd want at least one of us to work, just to be sure there would be a little security and something left to pass on to the children. So, maybe they have enough to own a fancy home but not enough to pay for life expenses. If you can't afford to do anything but stay in your nice home, life could still become pretty dull."

Jeff grinned. "If you ever experience it, let me know."

Minutes later, he pulled to a stop directly in front of a large cluster of sage bushes.

He threw a thumb over his shoulder. "I don't think anyone can see us up here. I packed snacks. We can eat during surveillance."

"Oh."

She noticed his arm strain against his sleeves as he reached behind her for the bag. Her mind flashed to her brother Nate's Hulk cartoons, right before the doctor transformed into the green superhero. She looked away and tried not to laugh. "How old were you when you last wore that shirt?"

Jeff stopped stretching for the bag and glanced down. Was he blushing? He grinned sheepishly. "Probably just before I started business school. Aunt Katie didn't keep much after I moved out."

She opened the passenger side door. "I'm counting on you to keep an eye out for wild animals. This city girl doesn't have much pepper spray left."

He winked. "Deal."

They were parked on a plateau of one of the hills. Long grasses waved, as if cheering silently that they had company. She couldn't see any of the houses below from this vantage point. "That rock over there looks flat enough to sit on."

"More like a boulder."

"A rock is a boulder."

He swung the bag over his shoulder. "Not unless you call it a *big* rock. That one is almost big enough to qualify for bouldering."

"You're making that up," she said.

He joined up with her. "No, ma'am."

"What is bouldering?" She lost her footing, tripping on a softball-size rock. He grabbed her arm, saving her from a face-plant.

Jeff shrugged but didn't let go of her, leading her through the terrain. "It's like rock climbing without as much equipment. You go small distances, focus on climbing, and don't usually wear any harnesses. Sometimes there's a mat to land on."

"You've tried it?"

He nodded as they reached the rock...boulder. "Yes, but not really my thing. Obviously skydiving is my passion."

"Did you always have a passion for extreme sports?"

He frowned. "Not that I can remember. It wasn't until I moved to the city. Skydiving helped me feel...I don't know, alive. Working at a factory and sitting at a desk in school was so different from working on the farm."

Her daily walks with Baloo did the same thing for her. She would let her mind and imagination run wild while Baloo led her down the path. "It's your escape," she guessed.

"Yes," he said quietly, staring into her eyes. "An outlet."

Victoria turned away. She used both hands and feet to hoist up to the flat spot on top of the boulder she saw from the road. A spattering of trees in front of them allowed them to see down below but gave enough coverage that she didn't feel conspicuous.

A sloping hill in front of them displayed wild purple lupine flowers. "Look at those dogwood trees down there. There, next to the Spanish-colonial stucco house."

"I think Wagner's house is the one next to it." The sun hung directly overhead, highlighting the clear blue sky and swaying prairie fields below. She accepted a water bottle from Jeff as he sat beside her, and scanned the neighborhood.

"Do you see the red Rover?"

"Not from this vantage point, but we will check again before we get closer." He opened the bag and pulled out a sandwich. "I think you'll find this has Aunt Katie's stamp of approval."

Victoria leaned over and peeked into the bag. "Whoopee pies!" She unwrapped the cookie-filled dessert and took a bite.

"You don't want your sandwich?"

"Oh, I do, but if this weekend has taught me anything, it's that life is too unpredictable not to eat dessert first!"

He laughed and opened his mouth, as if to ask her something, then quickly closed it.

"What?"

"Nothing."

"You can't do that," she teased. "It drives a person crazy. What is it?"

"You just have some filling stuck to the side of your mouth." His finger circled around the side of his own mouth.

Victoria turned away and tried to wipe it off. She turned back and found him staring at her, hard. She set the dessert down on the picnic bag and smiled. "It's still there, isn't it?"

"No," he said. "I'm thinking about what you said. Life is too unpredictable."

She shrugged. "I'm just trying to take your advice and live in the moment."

Not breaking eye contact, he leaned toward her. Her breath caught, and she recognized the promise of a kiss. Her heart raced. Her mind stopped working.

She closed the distance and wrapped both arms around his neck the moment his lips touched hers.

The wind whipped her hair to the side, and Victoria felt as if she was in the air again with him, flying, before…the reminder of their predicament felt like a bucket of cold water. She released her arms from him and jerked back, shaken.

Jeff looked pained. "Victoria, I… This isn't usually…" He cleared his throat. "I promise I don't…"

"I know," she interrupted and looked out at the flowers and grasses that grew still as the wind ceased. She couldn't bear to hear him apologize. Why had she let her guard down? Her heart ached to think she'd just thrown herself at him, a man known for a one-date limit.

"You know? What do you mean?"

She put a hand on her forehead to block the sun's glare and focused on the street below. "We're both under a lot of stress right now. We've been together nonstop for over twenty-four hours. Given the situation, we'd either have killed each other or felt irrationally close. That's all. Besides, it'd never work for us anyway. It's fine." She avoided making eye contact but reached for the picnic bag. "So, this sandwich is something amazing, huh?"

He said nothing, but she could feel him watching her. "Yeah," he said, his voice stern. He picked up his sandwich, still wrapped inside a bread towel.

Victoria squinted and willed herself to focus as hard as possible on her surroundings, minus Jeff. She needed to think straight, to keep her heart from getting involved.

"Don't know why I apologized then," Jeff muttered. "After all, you're the one that kissed me."

She gasped. "What?"

ELEVEN

He watched Victoria's cheeks flame before he turned away. "I won't deny I was thinking about it," he admitted. "But I was surprised when you…" He couldn't finish his thought aloud. He already regretted saying a thing. He should've left it alone, but his stupid pride was getting the best of him.

He heard her stand up. "I think we better agree to disagree and leave it at that."

Jeff's stomach churned. His taste buds didn't even truly register Aunt Katie's turkey, roast beef, bacon, French bread sandwich with garlic mayonnaise slathered on both sides. All he could think about was the sweet taste of Victoria's lips, whoopee pie-filling or not. The way her eyes met his with such loving kindness as she reached both arms fully around him, and pulled him closer. A split second later, she'd bolted.

He took a ragged breath. "Wagner's house is the mini-mansion with the white pillars." He pointed. "Looks like the garage door is open." He slid off the boulder and walked up to one of the large maple trees. Keeping one hand on it for support lest he slide down the steep terrain, he peeked around the bark for a better look.

A block to the left he saw a silver muscle car. He stepped back, into the shadows behind a cluster of sage. "That car…I think that was the car I saw in Drake's subdivision."

Victoria joined him in the shadows, on her toes with her neck craned. "Are you sure? We're pretty far away up here. There are a lot of silver cars out there. I can think of two cars exactly like that in my subdivision alone." She cleared her throat. "Doesn't April have a car like that?"

Jeff couldn't take his eyes off the vehicle. "I…I'm not sure. When we went to dinner, I drove." Something was bothering him. A vague memory that he couldn't place prompted the beginnings of a headache. He grunted. "But just to be safe, I don't want us to drive down there and make our presence known. I think a change of plans is in order." He turned to her. "I'm going to hike down to talk to him, and I want you to stay here. It's the safest option."

She glared at him for a half second before moving but said nothing. As they hastily cleaned up, their hands brushed against each other not once but twice. Victoria jerked back each time with an unnecessary apology that made his blood boil.

He gritted his teeth. Served him right for kissing her. Jeff wanted to kick the car tires, but he didn't want to give her the satisfaction of knowing that she affected him that much.

Jeff pointed out the rifle behind the truck's seats. "I don't have pepper spray, but Uncle Dean let me take one of his rifles he uses to keep the coyotes at bay. You know how to use a gun?" She shrugged, and he took it as a yes. "It's loaded with one bullet, but there are more in the box underneath the seat if you need them. I'll be as fast as I can." He handed her the keys. "Just in case things go south."

She nodded and shoved her hands into her pockets. She was still mad at him. "Victoria, I know you think I don't plan ahead, but believe it or not, I excel at it as a supervisor and even as a skydive instructor." He cringed. He hadn't exactly proven his point with his last dive. He'd already explained that, though, and didn't want to start another argument. "What makes me successful is the ability to be flexible when things don't go according to plan. It's another reason I think it's best I go in alone."

She pursed her lips and ripped off the page from her legal pad. "At least take this with you if you need help knowing what to ask him."

Jeff accepted the page and stuffed it in his pocket. Why did she insist on doing everything as a team? Some things were just better to do alone. He grabbed his phone and left without another word. He slipped the battery back into place and shoved the phone in his back pocket without looking at it. He needed to focus on the terrain. He hiked down the steep curves, grabbing the occasional tree to steady his balance now and then. At the bottom, he strode purposefully to Wagner's driveway. His neck prickled as if he could feel Victoria's eyes watching him above. He dared a glance up. He really had chosen a good hiding place. He couldn't see her or the truck.

The garage was still open as well as the trunk of a platinum Cadillac CTS. While it was definitely Wagner's car, it surprised him to see his boss had left the trunk open with a leather Samsonite suitcase sitting in it. Clearly, crime must not be of concern in the elite neighborhood. But where was his boss going?

He walked up the long curved pathway to the white

pillars holding the roof over the porch. Jeff gawked at the massive size of the house. There was no way Wagner had enough kids to justify such square footage.

He lifted his hand to knock, but the door was just slightly ajar. *Ah, so that's why the trunk was left open. He is going in and out.* Jeff turned around and gazed at the two evergreens on either side of the house, essentially providing the home with privacy from the only main road in and out of the foothills. The question was, should he just wait out here for Wagner, or his wife, to step back out again, or should he knock?

He took the third option and rang the doorbell. A full minute passed. He used his foot to kick at the door slightly. After all, it wasn't closed. He stuck his head in and found the front room—with wooden floors, an oriental rug, antique furniture and vaulted ceilings—to be utterly empty. "Mr. Wagner? It's Jeff Tucker from the office. I really need to talk to you."

As if in response, he heard a large thud. "Mr. Wagner?" he shouted.

The back of his neck tightened, an unsettling tingle grew from the base of his neck and ran down his spine. Jeff followed his instinct and stepped into the room, calling out his boss's name over and over. He walked through the kitchen, dining room, living room and finally down a long hallway. Glancing in the first room to his right, he spotted a chair overturned in the office. The place had been ransacked. He turned to leave when he spied what looked like the tips of fingers beneath the desk.

"Mr. Wagner?"

He ran around the desk and found Wagner's body curled up on the ground, blood seeping into the white plush carpet. "Mr. Wagner!" Kneeling, he picked up

Wagner's wrist and found a faint pulse. As he lifted the arm, it became evident the blood came from a wound in the chest. He'd been shot. He pulled out his cell phone. No signal. Shoot. They should've checked that before splitting up.

Jeff lunged for the telephone on the desk, already off the hook. He placed the phone to his hear. "Hello?" Silence.

He clicked the receiver and, after hearing a dial tone, pressed 9-1-1. "Someone shot Todd Wagner. He needs medical attention right away."

When dispatch asked for the address, he shuffled through the envelopes until he found a return address to relay. He looked back at Wagner on the floor. "What do I do? Pressure on the wound?"

"I need you to stay calm and stay on the line, sir. Do you see the shooter? Is the shooter still there?"

"Um, no and no. I don't think so." He heard what sounded like a door closing in the far distance, but he couldn't be sure. His own heart was pounding so loud in his ears that he didn't trust himself. For once, he wished Victoria would ignore his directions and come inside and help. He should've never let his pride take over his mouth.

"What is your name?" the voice asked.

"Just tell me what to do!"

"I need your name, sir."

Jeff tried to pull the phone down with him to the ground but found the cord to be too short. He threw the phone down in frustration. He looked over at Wagner's body. What next? He held his hands over Wagner's body in an attempt to narrow his focus. If a skydiver were on the ground, gouged from something on the ground and bleeding, he'd know what to do. Jeff took a deep breath. *That's it! Breathing!*

Jeff threw himself down on his knees and placed his left hand between Wagner's nose and mouth. A small puff of air brushed against his skin. Good, there was airflow. Moving to his chest he unbuttoned the first three buttons of Wagner's dress shirt and used a dry part of the shirt to press down hard on the wound with both hands.

"Jeff?"

His eyes darted to Wagner's face. Pale, but eyes open, Wagner breathed fully out of his mouth.

"Hang with me. Stay still. Focus on breathing. The paramedics are on their way." Jeff looked back toward the phone. They better be on their way. He pulled out his cell phone with one hand and let out a growl of frustration. Surely Wagner had a cell phone that had a signal—from a different service? Maybe satellite? He checked Wagner's pockets with his left hand while keeping pressure on Wagner's chest with his right. Nothing.

"Ironic," Wagner whispered.

"That you're shot?" Jeff asked. "Yeah, I'm guessing that would be ironic for anyone. Conserve energy, Wagner." Hot liquid touched his hand. It oozed between the fingers of his right hand. He straightened up on his knees for greater leverage and pressed harder on the wound.

Wagner winced.

"Sorry. I know it hurts, but I need to slow the bleeding." He tried to peek over Wagner's back. "I don't see an exit wound."

Wagner eyes closed, rasped, "I told them not to kill you but...she kills me."

Jeff lightened up on the pressure, shocked at his words, then focused. "Who's behind this?"

Wagner gave an almost imperceptible shake of the head. "Tricked." He licked his lips.

"Help us, then. Who did this?"

Wagner swallowed hard, his eyes squinted tight, his face pale.

"Hang on. Just hang on. Where's your cell phone? Is your wife here?"

Wagner shook his head ever so slightly. "Left. Affair," he croaked.

At least that's what Jeff thought he said. He stared at Wagner's face. So much pain, and likely not just from the gunshot. "You can live through this. It's not too late to tell the truth."

"Able," Wagner whispered.

Jeff frowned. "Able to do what?"

Wagner began to shiver. "Danger." His teeth began to chatter. "Hi-hi-hide."

Jeff's arms began to shake at the pressure and weight of Wagner's words. Was he asking Jeff and Victoria to go on the run or accept a life in prison? "I'm trying to save your life here, Todd! Do the right thing! Tell me what I need to know."

Jeff was not going to take no for an answer. Except Wagner's shivers became violent shakes. Wagner coughed, and a fine mist of blood escaped his lips. Jeff reeled back, horrified. Had he pushed him too far? *Lord, please help! Send help!*

Victoria got out of the car to stretch her legs. She'd let Jeff go without a fight mostly because she was too embarrassed to argue, and needed a moment to get her head on straight. The little rant about his abilities irked her. Of course she knew he was competent. It was one of the reasons she went to him in the first place, but she didn't want him acting like a supervisor right now. She wanted him to be her partner in this, and right now, her partner was taking too long. What if Wagner was holding a gun and making him wait for the police? Would anyone believe them?

In addition, if she didn't like the answers Wagner gave Jeff, she might just have to go back in and have a turn herself. After all, Jeff may have claimed to understand the situation, but he hadn't been the one to notice the discrepancies in the first place.

Wanting another glimpse of the valley, she walked in the opposite direction of the houses. The sloping hill enabled her to see the garden behind the Veteran's Administration building miles below them. Ironic that it wasn't until her life was at stake that she experienced more of Idaho than she'd ever seen before. She'd always meant to go sightseeing but had just settled for her life falling into a rut instead of enjoying the freedom she took for granted.

She closed her eyes, intending to pray, but instead memories of the expense reports kept flashing in her mind. Those business names that had disappeared, they'd all had P.O. boxes for the checks to be sent. Where were there physical locations? Did the businesses even exist? Victoria's eyes flashed open. The expense reports may have been deleted, but what if the individual invoices from those companies were still in the system?

Victoria shook her head. Getting the chance to look for them was easier said than done. Except, this was the excuse she needed to go into the meeting with Jeff and Wagner. She would say she had evidence that the expenses didn't just disappear but were actually counterfeit. If Wagner squirmed, then she'd have her answer.

She hopped into the truck and drove down the steep incline, navigating the curves. If they needed to make a fast getaway, she didn't want to hike up the minimountain. Her legs were still sore from the hiking yesterday.

Victoria slowed the truck down to a crawl once houses appeared. Where to park? She drove past the silver car that gave Jeff so much grief. She did a double take at the license plate and braked. The combination of letters and numbers gave her heart a jolt. She swung the truck around, which gave her arm muscles quite the workout without power steering, and parked in front of the evergreen trees by the Spanish stucco house. She rustled through the items in the cab until she found her cell phone and the battery in the glove compartment. She reassembled it and pressed the power button. No signal registered this far up in the mountains but that didn't mean that her well-organized files wouldn't pull up. In her "Important Numbers" file on the phone she found her own license plate number. Her heart sped up. The silver car definitely held her license plates.

She closed her eyes and tried to remember every detail when she'd been at Jeff's apartment waiting for the bomb squad and police to check her car. Had they mentioned her license plate was missing? She couldn't remember but knew, without a doubt, someone had stolen it and put it on the silver car. No doubt the same person who put the bomb there in the first place. Why would they do that?

Her heart raced. She was about to be framed for something more than embezzling. Jeff had to be warned.

Victoria stepped onto the street and gawked at the sight of the massive house—at least what she could see behind the giant evergreen trees. A small trail of smoke snaked up from the back, far left of the house. Except, it didn't seem cold enough for a fireplace and there wouldn't be leaves to burn, unless someone burned their own trash. But if someone could afford a fancy house, why wouldn't they just pay the money for garbage service?

A door slammed. An elderly man walked into the adjacent yard, wearing gardening gloves. He walked right up to Uncle Dean's green truck and looked inside the window. People in the neighborhood probably weren't used to strange cars parking on the street. She waved, hoping he understood the gesture to be her claiming ownership.

He stared at her for a full second but didn't wave back. She pointed to the house in front of her and hollered, "Just waiting for my friend and then we'll be gone."

The man showed no recognition of her words. Instead, he lowered his head, walked over to the flower bed and leaned over a bush with what looked like small clippers in his hand. Jeff would be furious with her for letting the neighbors spot her and the truck.

She returned her attention to Wagner's house. The smoke from the back had grown thicker, darker and more pronounced. This time, she left her doubt behind and ran up the pathway. She hadn't seen the open doorway from the road. "Jeff?" she yelled, poking her head inside.

She quickly walked through the house in the direction she saw the smoke.

"In here!"

She followed the sound of Jeff's voice and entered the room, only to find his hands covered in blood. Her mind slowly registered that the man below him was Wagner, shot. She jumped back. "Jeff! What happened? Tell me you didn't."

"Of course I didn't!" he shouted back. He jerked his head behind him. "Make sure EMTs are on the way."

She ran across the room and stepped behind them, and over piles of papers on the floor. "We might have another problem. The house might be on fire and someone's trying to frame us for it." She gasped. "Or shooting Wagner!" She lifted the phone. "Are the EMTs coming?"

"Yes, ma'am. Can you tell me who is speaking?"

"The house may be on fire, too," Victoria said into the phone, intentionally ignoring the question. "I'm going to check now." As she turned to face Jeff, her eye caught something out of place. She faced the desk and studied the contents of a small, open black leather bag. "Passport and money orders?"

She looked down at Wagner, blood slowly dripping from his mouth, his eyes closed. Her stomach churned at the sight. She looked up at the ceiling, until the dizzy feeling passed. "Is he conscious?"

Jeff shrugged. "He was a minute ago. I can't leave him. You sure the house is on fire?"

Victoria took a deep breath and ran out of the room into the hallway. Every door remained closed in the corridor, all the way to the end of the house—the general direction where she spotted the smoke rising. She placed her hand on each door as she worked her way down the coffee-colored hallway. It was cool to the touch; she sniffed for half a second before continuing her inspections. She detected the vile smell of plastic and wood burning and knew a red Range Rover had to be hiding somewhere nearby.

A moment later she spotted tendrils of smoke like

monsters' fingers gripping the bottom of the door at the end of the hallway. The vines of smoke shot up the door and hit the ceiling.

TWELVE

Victoria froze, her mind wrestling with what to do next. "Fire!" She pivoted and ran back to Jeff.

His eyes wide, he looked up at her and back to Wagner. "How close?"

The smoke alarms, one by one, concurred with her story. She held both hands over her ears and ran to Jeff's side. "We have to get him out," she shouted. Unbidden images of her own house on fire swarmed her thoughts. "Now!"

He clenched his jaw and nodded. "I don't know if it's safe to move him! What if his spine—"

"We can't risk waiting." Victoria leaned down. "You get his torso, I'll get his legs. You have to let go of the wound for a moment."

"He's bleeding too fast! If I let go, I don't know if he'll make it."

Victoria looked at Jeff's shaking hands and was thankful Aunt Katie had provided her layers. She wore a navy cotton T-shirt underneath, so she pulled off the top blouse.

She stepped over Jeff and slid the shirt underneath Wagner's shoulder. He winced.

"Sorry," she said. She wasn't so much apologetic as relieved that his pain was confirmation that he was still alive. She bit her lip and tied the blouse diagonally so that the fabric dug into the flesh underneath his armpit.

"What are you doing?" Jeff asked. "How on earth is that going to help?"

"Pressure point," she said, pulling as tight as possible before tying a knot. Wagner released a low moan. Victoria coughed and gagged as the air in the room turned an opaque white. She looked up to find the smoke swimming its way into the room. "It's our best hope! We can't wait. Let's go!"

"Get in place, then." He motioned for her to move.

She obeyed and jumped over to Wagner's knees.

Jeff stood up halfway, still pressing on Wagner's chest. Finally he let go, placed one hand underneath Wagner's waist and the other underneath his neck. "One, two, three!" With a guttural growl, Jeff lifted.

The muscles in her hamstrings and back smarted as she obeyed. Wagner was not a lightweight. Side by side, they attempted to carry the man as one. She wondered why Jeff chose to carry him this way. It might have been easier if she took his feet and Jeff took his head, but that would mean his body would sag in the middle—probably not good for a gunshot victim.

Her arms shook as her small steps sideways led them through the room and to the hallway. She wanted to let go, to let Jeff take over, but she knew he couldn't be much better off. Her eyes began to tear. Her lungs burned, and she worried she might choke on her coughs while holding such a heavy load.

"Faster," Jeff croaked.

Victoria began counting her steps for motivation. She

could go five steps. She could do another five, squatting a little deeper with every step. She tucked her chin to her chest, hoping to draw in the cleanest oxygen possible while standing. Her eyes dared to dart down the hallway, but the air had turned to dark gray with hints of orange coming her way.

A current of heat hit her face. Her thighs began to tremble, and the sweat on her hands threatened to make her lose grasp of Wagner's knees. Jeff stood ramrod straight. His arms hit against her shoulder with every step. She wasn't moving fast enough.

The next step revealed they had made it to the first living room. "The couch," she croaked. "Please!"

Jeff seemed to understand her and swung Wagner's body around. She tried to gently lay Wagner on the cushions, but he fell the last few inches. For his sake, she was glad he was unconscious, but it made her all the more nervous he wouldn't make it out alive.

Coughs racked her lungs, but she couldn't afford to stop. She grabbed the armrest of the love seat and shoved while Jeff pulled. The couch slid along the wooden floor. Jeff lifted it over the small threshold into the hallway. Victoria did her best to match his strength, shoving while her shoes pressed into the hallway carpet. She had to get the couch over the bump. With a snap, the wooden legs holding up her end of the couch dropped to the ground.

A sudden burst of heat struck her back. She chanced a look over her shoulder. The flames licked the hallway walls. The air was turning black and coming their way. Jeff raised his shoulders up, then yanked. He let out a roar from the effort, as he pulled her, along with the couch, over the incline.

The momentum flew them across the dining room

floor. She guided the broken end around the corner, and Jeff pulled with a speed she couldn't match. Victoria slid—along with the couch—all the way across the foyer's wooden floors. Jeff looked out the front door. "We have to carry him again. Can you do it?"

Her body wanted her to scream a refusal, but logically she knew there was no other way. The couch was too big to fit through the front door without putting it on its side. Wagner's head was facing the door. Jeff took the lead, once again picking him by the waist and neck. Victoria grabbed his knees again. *Please, Lord, help us get him out without damaging his spine.*

Jeff looked at her briefly. "Now!"

She was sure the muscle fibers in her abdominals were starting to rip. She couldn't stand the pain of holding up the man's considerable weight much longer. With a final surge of adrenaline, she rushed after Jeff through the doorway. He stepped off the patio and, mercifully, led them onto the grass on the side, avoiding the cement stairs leading down to the driveway. "Help us," Jeff shouted at the elderly neighbor.

The gardener jogged over just as a neighbor two houses down—a fit salt-and-pepper gentleman—stepped out his door and sprinted over. He took Victoria's burden. She croaked her thanks, her voice unable to carry far. The men didn't stop moving Wagner until they reached the adjacent yard. The flames had reached the outside of Wagner's house, visible to all now. Catching a glimpse of the hose reel beside the elderly gardener's home, Victoria darted to it.

Her hands stung from the effort of carrying her boss, so Victoria pulled out her ponytail elastic from her pocket and slipped it over the sprayer handle—to let it do the work—then turned on the hose. She turned the black iron crank that housed the tubing with her other hand, feeding foot upon foot of hose to the ground. She aimed the stream of pressurized water at the side of Wagner's house that wasn't burning yet. Convinced it was at least somewhat wet, she turned around and pointed it at the siding of the elderly man's house. Wagner's house may have no hope left, but in the dry weather, the rest of the houses could go up like a box of matchsticks.

The blissful sound of emergency sirens reached her ears. Help was most definitely on its way. The elderly man appeared at her side and reached for the hose. "Thank you," he said, his voice shaky and his eyes determined. He took her place to continue dousing his home with water.

Jeff jogged toward her. "Victoria!" He grabbed her hand and pulled her down the yard toward the truck, past the fit man who had taken over the duty of pressure to the wound. "Help is on the way. We need to leave before the police get here."

Victoria did as she was told, looking over her shoulder at the tragedy all around. "But…"

Bang.

She instinctively ducked. Her right eardrum throbbed, as if it had cracked a bit. What had just happened? Jeff's face was white. He grabbed her hand and pulled her into the vehicle. "Someone's shooting at us."

Jeff started the engine and pressed the gas. He had to get Victoria to safety. He heard another shot. This time it sounded as if it hit the bed of the truck.

"Are you sure it's at us?" Victoria looked back through the rearview mirror.

"Stay down!" He reached over and put his hand on Victoria's back, trying to help her slide from sight while he pressed the accelerator as far as it would go. A high-pitched crash sounded before a stinging sensation spread all over his neck. Had he been shot?

A gush of air rushed past his neck, and his hair blew down his forehead. The rearview mirror was covered with little sparkling bits but not enough to hide the fact that the rear window had been shot, shattering glass throughout the car.

Jeff barreled through the curves they had just navigated minutes ago. Instead of following the lines and staying within their own lane, he drove as diagonal as he could, slicing through the curves.

He kept both hands on the steering wheel. Jeff hoped that the shooter was still back at the house. *Please, protect Wagner and those men, Lord.*

Perhaps from the smoke or shock, Victoria remained silent.

"Are you okay?"

She still had her head low, by her knees. She shook her head and glass rained down from her hair. She sat up slowly with something in her hand.

"What? What is it?"

She wordlessly opened her hand. Inside was a gun shell.

"It went through the corner of the seat," she said. She stared at it. "I think it missed me by an inch." Victoria spun around and looked out the back, where the window used to be. "What happened back there?" she cried, inciting another fit of coughing.

He shook his head and choked a cough, too. "Water?"

She gasped. "You're bleeding on your neck. Were you shot?"

He shook his head and did his best to ignore the sharp stinging from his neck. If he put his hand back there without seeing what he was dealing with, he might make the glass go in deeper. "I think it's from the shattered glass."

She grabbed the picnic bag from behind his seat and passed Jeff a water bottle. She gulped down her own until it was empty. He started to drink but stopped when he noticed the sticky blood on his hands. Wagner's blood. He couldn't think about that now.

They drove in silence other than drinking and coughing for minutes. The sound of sirens no longer could be heard. Either the EMTs and firefighters had made it to the neighborhood, or Jeff and Victoria were already too far away.

"How fast are you going?" she asked.

Jeff sped past the intersection to the highway. "You missed it," she objected. He didn't answer her, and she leaned forward trying to catch his eye. "Did you hear me? You missed it!"

Two blocks later he made a hard left; the back side of the truck slid across the gravel. "We're taking side roads back," he said.

Victoria flung open the glove compartment.

"What are you doing?"

"Looking for something. Please, be there. Yes!" She grabbed his arm and let go when he flinched. "Pull over. Now."

THIRTEEN

Victoria gritted her teeth, when, instead of slowing, the truck seemed to give a kick before going even faster.

"I don't think we should stop. Wagner said he tried to keep her from killing us, but then she killed him." He gripped the wheel.

"Wait. She?"

He barked a harsh laugh. "Some warning. You could've easily died with the fire and then the bomb. And now we have a markswoman out to kill us."

"That doesn't make sense. I know it was a man who set my house on fire. I'm certain. Jeff, did Wagner say who it was? Did he give you a name?"

"He wouldn't talk, Victoria. First he said he was able, but then he said we were in danger, and we needed to hide."

"Wagner said we should hide?"

"Just before he lost consciousness."

A sick feeling in her gut prompted her to drop her head in her hands. "What if…what if that day Wagner ordered me to meet him after work, I mistook him trying to help for advances?"

"Either way he was part of this, and you were right not to trust him."

Jeff's words were reassuring, but Victoria was starting to question her ability to read people—first with Jeff and now Wagner. She'd convinced herself she could interpret motives by facial expressions. Was it pride assuming she could analyze people that way? Or worry disguised as pride?

Victoria noticed white streaks all over Jeff's face, like rain running down a window. He was covered in soot. She looked down at her shirt, now ashen. Her eyes began to itch. She lifted the inside seam and tried to wipe her eyelids. Black grime.

"Guess you were right. You should've come in with me from the outset. I couldn't have gotten him out without you. And I...I don't know what I would've done if you'd been shot."

She threw her hands up in the air. "But who shot him, Jeff? What happened?"

"I know as much as you know!" He wrenched the wheel to the right, and the truck bolted up a small dark mud trail until a rustic wood structure came into view. Jeff guided the truck behind it and came to a screeching halt.

"Where are we?"

"A snowmobile warming hut. We're not visible from the road anymore." His forehead fell into his right hand—now covered in dried blood—as his body began shaking.

She reached over and placed her hand on his shoulder. At least he had finally pulled over. "You saved Wagner's life."

He looked up and out through the window, his eyes red with restrained emotion. "I hope you're right."

She looked down at her lap at the red first aid kit she'd found. "Get out of the car. I need to remove the glass shards. Take off your shirt."

For once, Jeff didn't argue. Another signal he must be in shock. She hopped out of the truck, as he exited from the driver's side. She grabbed the last water bottle from the picnic bag and ran to him. His button-down shirt hung from the side mirror. She wondered if she'd need him to take off his undershirt as well, but the suggestion froze on her lips. Maybe she'd leave Aunt Katie to do the more thorough check. "Just bend over and hang your head down, okay?"

The blood flowed from the array of small and big cuts on his neck. "This might sting." In her right hand, she held the tweezers found in the first aid kit. With her left, she poured a small amount of water over his neck. The blood dissipated for a moment, and she could see five ragged pieces of glass embedded. She worked rapidly with the tweezers. She flung each splinter to the side. "If you didn't make sure I stayed down, we'd both be covered in glass," she mused.

The full weight of his actions hit Victoria. Jeff had once again sacrificed for her. "In fact," she said, barely over a whisper, "if you hadn't shoved my head down, my knees wouldn't have moved to the right, and I'd probably have a bullet lodged in my calf."

He didn't reply. The memory of Jeff's accusation that she'd kissed him caused her cheeks to heat and her stomach to feel hot. She cleared her throat. "So much for assuming we wouldn't need to deal with guns, right?"

"And we have more than one person trying to kill us. We know of two. The question is…are there more?"

Her fingers shook a little at his words. She took a

deep breath. Twice more she poured water on his neck. He groaned but let her work.

"That's all I can see for now." She lifted his shirt off the mirror. "Tell Aunt Katie sorry for me, but I don't have any large bandages. I think the blood might have ruined this shirt anyway." She ripped the sleeve off the shirt, then turned the sleeve inside out so the soot wouldn't be against his wounds.

He stared at her, his eyes darkening. He dried his neck off with the sleeve, then took the remainder of his shirt and swept out the glass from his seat. He offered it to Victoria for her to do the same on her side. "I'm sorry," he said, his voice husky. "It was my idea to go to Wagner, and it just made things worse."

"He would've died if we hadn't gone," she said softly.

He rocked back on his heels and looked at the sky. "I hadn't thought of it that way."

"Being shot at wasn't part of the plan."

Jeff leaned against the outside of the truck. He'd had to carry much of Wagner's body weight, and he looked spent, weary. Whether a good or bad guy, Wagner had worked closely for years with Jeff. It was no wonder Jeff was shaken to the core. Victoria had never liked the man, but she still prayed that he survived.

He grabbed a bag from behind the driver's seat. "I brought us an extra change of clothes. There's a room inside where we can change and go from there." He pulled out the rifle and let it hang at his side as he walked away from the warming hut and toward a group of rough-barked trees.

"Where are you going?"

"If you want to know, join me."

The gravel crunched underneath her feet. Under the

canopy of bare branches, he went to the far side of the biggest oak, then turned and stared at it. "Sometimes it's hard to find it in this light."

As if she was seeing an optical illusion, her eyes went from noticing nothing but bark to suddenly spotting a small, four-inch tall chunk missing from the tree. She reached her hand out and jerked back at the feel of metal.

"Ah, you found it. Great." Jeff lifted a key off the worn hook. "It used to be easier to find, but once everything weathered, it turned into a bit of a challenge."

"How do you know about this place?"

"A snowmobile club is responsible for maintaining it all year. My uncle used to volunteer me to help. I thought it was punishment for something I didn't understand, until years later. He volunteered me so I could get the chance to ride on the back of someone's snowmobile."

He put a hand on the makeshift bandage covering his neck and pressed down. "They keep five gallons of potable water inside at all times. Let's wash up and figure out the next step. We will have warning before someone comes up here, but I don't think it's safe to stay in one place very long."

"Maybe the police will find out who shot Wagner and, in the process, find out who framed us."

Jeff said nothing, just clenched his jaw and stared forward. Victoria sighed and prayed for wisdom in what to do next.

She had always relied on her plans and preparations in life, but what good had that done her thus far? Where were the fruits of her carefully planned life? She hadn't ended up an FBI agent and hadn't lived a safer existence as an accountant. Instead, she'd gotten the good, kind man next to her into an impossible situation. *What else do you have in store for us, Lord? Please, get us out of this mess.*

Jeff stood behind the large window in the warming hut. The adrenaline coursing through his veins moments ago disappeared. His neck stung, his eyes burned and he just wanted to sleep. Where should they go next?

He heard the door behind close and glanced over his shoulder. Victoria had washed up and changed into a pink button-down shirt and a fresh pair of jeans. She smiled, but it didn't reach her eyes. "You okay?" she asked.

He didn't know how to answer, so he turned back to the window. "I wasn't planning to return back to the house," he finally said.

"What? Why? Do you have somewhere else in mind?"

Jeff mulled over the past couple of days. He wanted to believe he'd acted wisely, but now he wondered if it was nothing but fear that had prompted his decisions. "I think there's something I need to tell you." Victoria faced him, but he kept his eyes on the window. "When I was seventeen, I skimmed off the till while I worked the counter at Tough as Nails Hardware. My boss knew my uncle and went to our church."

He tapped his fingers on the windowsill. "I promised him I would pay him every dime back, but before I could—" Jeff took a deep breath. He'd never told anyone of his secret shame. It was harder to talk about than he imagined.

Victoria raised her eyebrows. "Why'd you do it in the first place? It doesn't seem like the sort of thing you would do."

"I was a teenager with no impulse control. It was stupid and selfish. I thought the money would help me get a used truck a family in town was selling, before another guy in my class could snag it. But the moment my boss acted like he suspected, I came clean. I don't think he ever would've accused me outright, he wasn't that type of guy, but I couldn't sleep at night, and I couldn't look Aunt Katie or Uncle Dean in the eye for two weeks. So, at the time, it was a giant relief when I told him. He didn't yell, he just said he'd write up a loan contract on how I could pay him back. I'd have to work in the lumberyard instead of in the store at the register, and he'd need to tell my aunt and uncle."

Victoria nodded. "He sounds like a gracious man."

Jeff clenched his jaw. "He may have been, but Uncle Dean insisted that he press charges."

"He didn't do it, did he?"

"Stealing over a thousand dollars is considered grand theft," Jeff said slowly. "I served thirty days in prison."

"That...that must have been awful. How did you ever get a job after that?"

"I was technically still a juvenile. So, the judge granted that if I served my time and probation successfully, the charge would be stricken from my record. Except, the whole town knew about it. Victoria, if we need to defend ourselves against whoever is framing us, I know my past will come out. Not only will no one believe I'm innocent—" he turned to her "—they likely won't believe you, either."

Her eyes widened. "That's why you're so worried about being ethical at work...right down to the office pens."

"I'm not trying to prove anything, Victoria, but I do want to be a man of integrity."

She pursed her lips. "Did you have a hard time forgiving your uncle?"

He hadn't expected that question. Jeff looked down at his hands. Even though he'd used the jug of water to wash them, it felt as if they were stained with soot and Wagner's blood. "Yes, I forgave him. I couldn't understand why he wanted my boss to press charges when I had come forward and tried to make it right. Despite my good intentions, he was worried I would be tempted again if not dealt with harshly. He was afraid I'd turn into my real dad. And he thought I'd get one night in jail." He cleared his throat. "Not a month."

Jeff watched her face for any change in expression. What was she thinking of him now?

"I'm having a hard time understanding why that means we can't go back to the house, though." She put a hand on her cheek. "Wait. You think your uncle will turn you in? Us in?"

"I'm more worried about putting them in danger. Especially now that we're dealing with someone who doesn't mind hurting innocent bystanders while they try to kill us. But, yes, it's a possibility my uncle would turn us in."

Victoria brushed her hair back with her fingers. "I can't think of any other options at the moment." She turned toward him. "We haven't even been running for a full weekend, and I'm getting tired of it. I'm not cut out for this." She sighed. "Can we give them a chance? You're a responsible adult now. They clearly love you."

"Clearly, huh?" The stinging in the back of his neck returned.

"Yes, you saw them last night. They were so happy that you came back home."

"Victoria, no offense, but a couple of meals with them doesn't mean you know them. If they wanted to see me, why didn't they ask me to come visit them even once? Why didn't they once ask me about my life? Anytime we do visit, it consists of sharing presents or eating. On a rare day, they'd talk about what was going on at the farm."

Victoria jerked back.

"I didn't mean to raise my voice," he said.

"No, I get it," she said softly.

Jeff shook his head. "I told you to stop worrying, and I'm doing the same thing." He sighed. "I keep praying for wisdom, and I'm getting nothing."

"Maybe this time," she whispered, "we should ask together."

Jeff looked over at her outstretched hand. He turned his palm and accepted her invitation. He bowed his head, but remained wordless.

"Send help, Lord. Please." Her voice was soft, but her prayer was simple and exactly the words he was thinking.

Jeff looked up to find Victoria studying his face, still gripping his hand tightly. A rush of wind blew the warming hut door open. Her hair wild, her face still carrying a hint of soot, he found her just as beautiful as ever. He rubbed his thumb on the top of her hand, wanting to remain close to her. "Why would it never work? Is it because of our jobs?"

"No." She huffed a laugh. "I don't imagine we have jobs anymore. I mean, sure, if we did, you would be my supervisor, and it'd be out of the question. But a relationship wouldn't work despite that, so it's not an issue."

"Is it because of Nate?" he blurted. The moment the

words were out, he wished he could take it back. He dropped her hand like a hot potato.

Her eyes widened and her cheeks flamed, making her blue eyes seemed brighter. "Nate?" She seemed to be choking on a laugh. "No, Nate's my brother if you must know."

"I don't have to know. I only bring it up because he left you a text last night. Couldn't help but see it." Jeff recognized the chance to change the subject and attempt to repair the damage his words made. "Does he know what's going on?"

Her face fell. "No. We try to touch base every weekend. He has no idea about anything that's happened this week." She looked down at her shoes. "You've been searching all this time—on all your dates—for the elusive perfect woman. I'm not that. If I'm honest, a part of me wants to be that for you, but I'm tired of not living up to everyone's expectations and then getting my heart broken. I've done it too many times in my life. I can't do it again."

He narrowed his eyes. "You mean you can't take risks."

"Excuse me. I know the difference between a safe risk and a high risk."

He smirked. "If it was safe, it wouldn't be called a risk, Victoria."

Her mouth fell open. "Listen, I've seen what happens when risks are taken. I watched my parents invest everything into a sure thing and end up losing it all. I gave my heart to someone and he chose someone else. I reported a discrepancy just like the ones I found at Earth Generators at my first job, and what did it get me? An invitation to resign. And now? Well, you can see how well it's going, so excuse me if I don't want to take any more risks."

"And it was wrong what happened to your parents and you, but it doesn't mean you stop taking risks. Those things that happened weren't your fault. You didn't cause them to happen. You need to let it go."

Victoria turned forward. "You mean just like it wasn't your fault that your mother gave you up for adoption? That your aunt and uncle are your parents and love you like their own? Do you mean like that? Maybe you're the one who needs to let things go."

He narrowed his eyes. "Don't pretend you even know the half of it."

She flung her hands up in the air. "Since we apparently have nowhere to go, why don't you educate me?"

"Fine. Would you be able to let it go if your so-called adoptive parents wouldn't let you call them Mom and Dad growing up? Would you let it go if they never told you why your parents abandoned you? Would you?" The veins in his forehead and neck pulsed, bulging to the point of pain.

Victoria's face crumpled. The moment the accusing questions tumbled out of his mouth, he knew he had lost control. He'd never intended to talk about any old family business. "Victoria, I'm sorry. I don't know how we even—" He raked a hand through his hair. "I don't know what it is about you that makes me let my guard down."

"I'm sorry, too. I never meant to antagonize you." When her eyes met his, he could see the tears. "You hit a sore spot and I just—just retaliated. I'm sorry." She shook her head. "It's like we bring out the worst in each other."

An unbidden verse sprang to his mind. "Iron sharpens iron," he mumbled.

She looked up, surprised. "I...I guess so." She turned her gaze up to the clouds. "Yes, if I were you, I would have a hard time letting all that stuff go. But just like you pointed out for me, those things weren't your fault, either. And I'm sorry I pushed. It's not any of my business."

She kicked a pebble of gravel away. "I don't know what we're going to do." She dropped her head and placed her hands over her eyes.

Jeff walked up to her and pulled her hands away from her face and toward him. She stood and melted into his chest. He wrapped his arms around her and let his chin rest on the top of her head.

"You're right," he said, his voice hoarse. "I've never been under this much stress before. I'm letting things that normally wouldn't get to me drive me crazy." He looked out at the farmland to his left and right, the rows and rows of growing crops, the bright green color and open space bringing a sense of calm to his mind.

He wanted to tell her the truth about the kiss, but it didn't seem the right time. She'd see it as another player move, especially in this emotional state. In fact, she might think that about the hug. He took a deep breath and let her go.

Victoria bit her lip. "I'm thankful for you." She straightened, gave him a quick glance, then turned away and smiled softly. "The day is almost gone," she said.

"Wait. When you found me with Wagner, you said we were being framed. What did you mean by that?"

"Do you remember the silver car that looked familiar to you? I really hope you figure out where you last saw it, because it had my license plate on it."

"What? Why would someone do that? Your cars don't look anything alike."

"Think about it. If a witness takes the time to get a driver's license or even if they have surveillance video, what are they going to get out of it?"

"A silver car with your license plates."

She nodded. "Exactly. And the fact that we left Wagner at the scene makes us look even worse."

"It already looked bad with an obscene amount of money in our accounts."

"Sure. So what's a little arson and attempted murder to add to it? Is that what you're saying?" She held her hands together. "I just hope those neighbors tell the police we were trying to help."

"If they remember anything they'll remember the green truck." A surge of adrenaline spiked through his veins. He scooped up the backpack with their soiled clothes in it. "And the truck might lead them to my aunt and uncle! As much as I hate it, I need to warn them, and we need to get far away fast."

FOURTEEN

"**I** should have never brought the truck down where it could be seen." Victoria's insides burned. She could fight to live in the present moment as long as she wasn't reminded that someone wanted her dead. If her impulsive actions put Uncle Dean and Aunt Katie in danger, she wouldn't be able to forgive herself.

"Wagner and I would probably both be dead if you hadn't." Jeff took them down a very bumpy path, the opposite direction from where they had come. "This path eventually gets us to a road. We can't afford to be seen."

The wind from the broken back window sent chills down her spine. "Will Uncle Dean be mad about the window?"

"I doubt it. After the uh…incident, I couldn't so much as look at it. So I gave it to him to run around the farm. To this day he still says it's my truck and he's just keeping it ready for me when I want it." Jeff shook his head. "This thing has given me nothing but trouble. I'll never want it, especially now that it might put them in danger."

Victoria rubbed her temples. "Speaking of trouble, right before we got Wagner I figured out what we need to do next." She tilted her head from side to side. "I just have no idea how to do it."

Jeff turned his head slowly. "Oh?"

She relayed her idea on finding the invoices for the missing expenses. "It's a long shot, but maybe we contact the businesses, since I remember a few of them." She smiled. It gave her hope that someone else out there could provide the proof she needed.

Jeff slapped the steering wheel. "That's what was bothering me. I thought for sure we manufactured some of those parts ourselves. We certainly didn't have so many contractors with such idealized names! They even sound made up."

"Then why didn't you say something before?" she challenged.

"Because I wasn't sure."

"That's why you should speak your mind, Jeff," Victoria retorted, pointing her finger at him. Except, the last time Jeff had spoken his mind she couldn't handle it. She still hadn't fully processed their discussion at the warming hut. It made her want to laugh that he thought Nate was a threat. Nate…why hadn't she thought of it before? "Do you think we have a cell signal now?"

"I've kept my phone off on purpose. Feel free to try it, but keep it short."

To Victoria's relief her phone responded with a series of chimes when she powered it up. She scrolled through the useless text messages of people wanting to know where she was and what was going on. "I've worked with these people for how long, and while I could tell you all about them, do you know this is the first time they've ever asked me anything?"

"It's because you care," Jeff answered. "People like to talk about themselves. Most of them don't have anyone in their lives willing to listen. You know how to have

a meaningful two-way conversation. That right there
makes you a rarity in this world. I'm sure it never oc-
curred to them to ask you questions." He gave her a quick
glance. "Now that police are snooping around, you're
their ticket to the hottest gossip at work."

Victoria absorbed his words as the farmhouse came
into view. The front landscape boasted lilac trees and
even more flowers than the backyard. "I just wanted to
be their friend. You make it sound like I was offering
a service."

"More like a lifeline. People light up when you walk
in the room, Victoria. I thought you knew that."

She wanted to hide, but the only way she could con-
tain her feelings was to shift her focus. "I need to text
Nate," she said, hoping that would end the conversation.

Nate, sorry I haven't called. Life is nuts right now. If a
company lost their data would they typically keep a
backup somewhere else on the network?

"They'll see us coming," Jeff said, and turned into
the long driveway. "I need to park the truck somewhere
not visible to anyone else. Do you want me to drop you
off at the house first?"

"No, I'll walk with you," she answered. She didn't
want to be the first one to interact with Aunt Katie or
Uncle Dean. The awkwardness would lead her to spill
everything, and she really needed Jeff to be left with
that responsibility.

Her phone chimed again.

Glad u texted. Was getting worried. Yeah. Best Practices
require an off-site backup server in case corporate has
a fire or something. Ask the company IT guy.

She held up the phone. Jeff slowed the truck and read it over, and a slow grin erupted. "There's hope, then. Praise God. We needed some encouragement right about now."

He drove them over the same rocky terrain that she had run through just that morning before finding him next to his dog's grave. It seemed like a lifetime ago. He drove past the barn and underneath a pair of tall maple trees. "It should be well-hidden here."

"Do you know anyone in the IT department that we could ask for help?"

He got out of the truck and pulled his cell phone out of his pocket. She walked around the front of the car to join him. His finger scrolled down the screen. "I don't have anybody in my contacts from IT, but I have April in Human Resources. I figure she has everyone's number in her phone."

"Why would you think that?" Victoria sighed. Yes, they'd already established he had April's phone number. But it still stung that April had been checking on Jeff but had never bothered to ask her how she was doing. Some friend she'd turned out to be.

"Her office phone is linked to her cell phone. The IT guys set it up for most of the department heads. I know Wagner's is set up that way, too. She keeps her contacts linked to her smartphone."

He glanced at Victoria. She stood rigid with both hands clasped together. He held out the phone to her. "Unless you want to call her?"

She shook her head and took a step back. "No, I think she'd rather hear from you."

"Not due to any encouragement from me." He pressed April's number. "I'll put it on speakerphone."

"You don't have to for my benefit," she answered, but Jeff just held up a finger over his mouth.

April answered on the first ring. "Jeff, I've been wondering where you've been. Do you know the police are looking for you? Let me know how I can help."

Something seemed off. Her tone seemed saccharine. She was willing to help them despite the police looking for them?

"It's a misunderstanding I'm working on clearing up," Jeff replied. "You told me once you had the whole company directory in your smartphone. I'm wondering if you could help me out and give me Garrett's number?"

"Oh!" Her bubbly, loud voice caused Jeff to hold the phone at arm's length. She couldn't help but silently laugh at his reaction. Jeff cleared his throat and seemed to be fighting a smile.

"I would," April continued, "but the thing is…my phone synced wrong the other day, and beyond that, I just don't have everyone's number anymore. Is everything okay? Maybe if you tell me a little about the situation, I could help. I happen to be pretty handy with computers myself."

The one-way conversation wasn't helping. Jeff shook his head for Victoria's benefit. "That's okay. I won't keep you. Thanks, April. Bye."

"So, another dead end," Victoria mused. "She sounded kind of…off."

"She did." He scrolled through his list of contacts. "Let me try Bill."

"From our department?"

"It's a long shot, but I thought I remember him saying he plays Frisbee golf with Garrett in tournaments on the weekends. Frisbee golf was never really my thing, but to each his own." He pressed his name, and they listened to it dial. "Say a prayer," he whispered.

Bill did, in fact, have Garrett's number, but it took ten minutes to find a tactful way to end the phone call. Bill wanted to know who'd blown up Jeff's car. "It was all over work, man. Garrett and I needed to leave during lunch to make the tournament in Oregon. Who could have a vendetta against you? You're the nicest guy in the office. Oh, what if it's a lady gone mad for you?"

Jeff turned a shade of crimson. If Victoria hadn't seen it with her own eyes, she wouldn't have believed it. He closed his eyes and interrupted Bill's rant. "I'm sure it's not that. Thanks for your time, Bill. Got to go."

He ended the call. "Did you get that number?"

She pointed to the contact on her phone. "Right here."

He looked over her shoulder. "Thank you." He typed in the phone number. "I think I'll take it off speakerphone, if you don't mind."

"Worried you'll hear more theories about the *Jeff Tucker Dinner Club* going mad?" she teased.

He took in a deep breath, and his face flushed once more. "I'm going to pretend I didn't hear that."

Victoria laughed just as her own phone chimed three times. She'd forgotten to turn the cell service back off since texting her brother. The three messages were from Darcy, her neighbor.

Vic, what is going on? Your friend April was in your house.

She said police think you and your supervisor torched your house and his car for insurance money but got caught. You shot your boss and are on the run? This can't be true!

April tried to find evidence to help you but I'm afraid

everything in your house is destroyed. Let me know how I can help. I know this must all be a mistake. Praying 4 U!

Victoria's legs lost their strength, and she sank against the green truck. What on earth? Could it be true—how could the police think she set her own house on fire for the insurance money? She frowned and shook her head, wishing the motion would physically sort her thoughts into something that made sense.

Hadn't she just been thinking that April really wasn't that good a friend? If she had been at her house searching for evidence to clear them, why hadn't she mentioned that to Jeff a mere moment ago?

And she'd mentioned to Darcy that they were wanted for shooting their boss? They'd found Wagner shot only hours ago. Would it really be on the news already or was there another reason April knew? What if she was there?

Victoria gazed into the tree branches. The sunlight filtered through the leaves and for a brief moment resembled glistening diamonds suspended in the air. Diamonds... April loved her bling, always dressed to the nines. She had always assumed it was well-made costume jewelry, but what if it was the real thing? What if what April really had wanted was to find out if the flash drive in her house was destroyed?

"Garrett, I'm so glad to catch you, man. I need to ask you—if something were deleted from the corporate office, do we have a back-up server?"

Garrett laughed. "Jeff, what happened? I'm gone half a day and the place falls apart? Wait—" his voice sobered "—is this about your car exploding? Did something else happen? Is that why HR just called five minutes ago asking me the same thing?"

Jeff's breathing grew shallow. "Uh…I'm not sure. When you say HR, do you mean April?"

"Yeah."

Jeff's mind raced. What logical reason could April have for calling Garrett? She either lied about not having his phone number or…or nothing. There was no other reason he could fathom. "Could you tell me what you told her?"

"Yeah, no problem. The bottom line is that it depends on a number of factors. If it was saved on the server, however, then depending on how long ago it was first created, it's likely available on the backup server."

Jeff did his best to focus on Garrett's mind-numbing explanation. He didn't have time for so many details. "Where and how do you get the backup files?"

"Our company uses a local security firm called Data-Crypt. Our data goes to a cloud drive and then a few seconds later to DataCrypt's tape drives. So, you'd need to go physically there and use a tape drive to—"

"And you told all this to April?"

"Yeah, but she interrupted me at the same place you did only to hang up on me. If she'd have let me finish, I'd have told her there's an on-site backup at the office, too."

Jeff took a deep breath. His instinct told him to cut off Garrett and drive like a madman into town, but the very fact that April had hung up on Garrett prompted Jeff to continue listening. "Tell me more," he said.

"This can't wait until tomorrow? My wife just made me baked Alaska to celebrate my tournament win."

"I'm afraid it can't wait."

Garrett called out to his wife that he'd be just a few more minutes, and then he complied.

After receiving a minor lecture on IT servers and best

practices, Jeff owed him a small explanation. "Straight up, Garrett, we're in some trouble, but we didn't do anything wrong. I need to find the initial quarterly report and expense sheets Victoria submitted a couple of weeks ago. It'll make all the drama go away."

Only the sound of returning cicadas to the land around him hit Jeff's ears. For a moment, he wondered if the connection had broken. Heart pounding, he asked, "Are you there?"

"Yeah. I'm thinking." Garret released a long sigh. "Okay, listen. Not many employees are given the rights to access the server. You know Bill?"

Jeff huffed. "I'm his supervisor. He's the one that gave me your number."

"Okay, well, you didn't hear this from me, but the IT department may have granted Bill rights to access the server since he's constantly deleting his own work by accident. We got tired of retrieving it for him."

"Are you kidding me? You can give Bill admin rights, but not me?"

"I don't make the rules, Jeff. There are channels, checks and balances, a process—I can't just grant you that even if I wanted to. It takes time. Besides, Bill can only retrieve—not change anything—on the server. He doesn't have full admin rights."

Jeff clenched his left fist. "Bill can't even remember his password from week to week. I even have it for safekeeping because we got tired of issuing him new log-ins."

"Sounds to me like you have your answer, then," Garrett said, with a laugh. "But DataCrypt is the easiest solution. They can help you get what you want. I can't help you until Monday. Between you and me, Bill had a car accident a couple years ago. He's still a brilliant guy, but the blow to his head made his short-term memory a joke, so take it easy on him, okay? In fact, let's just pretend I have the same problem regarding this conversation."

Jeff grinned. God certainly did work in mysterious ways. "Fair enough, Garrett. Fair enough."

He hung up and gazed down at Victoria, who looked as if she might throw up. "Are you okay?"

"April," she croaked. She held out her cell phone.

He took it and read the text messages from Victoria's neighbor. "The way…the way you just said her name it was almost as if you said, 'able.' When I asked Wagner who was behind it all, he said, 'able.'" Jeff handed back the phone. "Reply and ask her what kind of car April was driving."

Victoria blinked as if waking up from a dream. "What?"

"Please."

She complied, and Jeff reached for her hand. "We need to keep moving. Garrett told me where the backup server is, and it's located near the airport. Problem is, April also knows."

"She's really behind this all?" she asked, breathless. A chime prompted them both to freeze and look down at the phone.

Silver sports car.

Victoria's wide eyes met his. "That's why the car was familiar to you." She looked down at the ground, as if searching for something. "But why? And who was the man following me and rifling in my car?"

"We don't have time to figure it out right now. I need to warn my aunt and uncle, and then we need to beat April before she gets her hands on our only chance to clear our names."

They reached the porch, and Victoria hung back. "I assume you want to talk to them alone?" she asked.

His shoulders sagged. "If you don't want to go in there with me, I understand. But, no, I'd rather you be with me." He was surprised the words came out of his mouth. The thought of disappointing his aunt and uncle again, the possibility of them not believing him, scared him more than he'd like to admit, but for whatever reason, Victoria gave him courage.

She nodded and stepped forward. "We're in this together," she said and followed him inside.

Aunt Katie stood at the kitchen counter, stirring a dish. "I thought I saw you coming down the drive a while ago. Just in time for dinner. Dean," she called.

Uncle Dean stepped in the kitchen. "Did you get sorted out whatever needed sorting?"

Jeff smiled. It was Uncle Dean's way of showing he cared without prying, but it was also the opening Jeff needed. "No, I'm afraid things have gotten much worse. The worst being that I've inadvertently put you in danger." Jeff explained the events of the past couple of days. "Bottom line. If the wrong people trace the truck, then you're not safe here."

Aunt Katie put both hands over her mouth, her eyes betraying her shock. Uncle Dean folded his arms over his chest and frowned. "What's the plan?"

Jeff took a step back. He imagined many scenarios of how Uncle Dean might have reacted to the news, but this was not one of them. "You believe me?"

Uncle Dean pursed his lips and shook his head. "Jeff," he said, his voice strained. "I have regrets. But the one thing I will never regret is raising you. You are not your dad. You are your own man. I've watched you grow into a man of God. I'm proud of you, and I can see you've done nothing wrong." He gestured to Victoria. "You both love the Lord, and I don't want these people messing with the plans God has for your lives. And I'm sure your aunt agrees with me."

Aunt Katie nodded, tears in her eyes. She pulled Jeff into a hug as Uncle Dean asked, "Now, how can we help?"

Uncle Dean's words kept playing over and over in her head. Jeff wasn't his dad; he was his own man, a man of God. *And he's not Blake.* She gulped. Katie interrupted her thoughts by putting an insulated bag in her hands.

"Food and plenty of water." She wrapped her arms around Victoria and gave her a squeeze.

"What about you two?" Victoria asked.

"I've been wanting to take a little vacation anyway. We'll celebrate our fortieth anniversary in McCall. It's supposed to be very romantic there." Katie grinned, then guided her to where Jeff was loading the back of a white Ford truck.

Victoria hung back while his uncle and aunt gathered close to him, speaking hushed words. Katie squeezed both of Jeff's hands together. "I'm not worried." She reached over and hugged him tightly, raised herself on her tiptoes and said, "God be with you, Jeffrey."

"And also with you," he answered. Victoria wondered if she'd just seen a glimpse of Jeff's childhood. Uncle Dean placed his large hand on Jeff's shoulder. One squeeze later, Jeff was behind the wheel and they drove into the darkening night, side by side.

FIFTEEN

Victoria wrapped her arms around herself. "I miss Baloo already. It feels like I'm abandoning him."

"You're not," Jeff said firmly.

She bit her lip. *Talk about sticking her foot in her mouth. If anyone knew what true abandonment felt like...* "I didn't mean—"

"I know." He smiled.

Her heart warmed.

"Now we need to focus on the next step ahead."

"We need to stop April is what we need to do," Victoria replied. "I can't believe it was her! She acted like my friend and...and your friend, too. Think. What do we know about her?" Victoria combed her memory. "She loves cats, movies, shopping and planning dream vacations." She stared at her four fingers. That's all she had?

Jeff curled his lip. "Did you have anything in common with her? I thought you said she was your friend."

"What do you mean?"

"You like dogs, reading, saving money and cooking at home."

It seemed the temperature had increased ten degrees. "Wow." He was right, but she wanted to know how he knew all of that about her.

He shrugged before she could ask. "Our miniconversations over the years added up. I know a few things about you."

Victoria put a hand on her chest and looked forward out the window. She waited a second for her heartbeat to slow. "April was one of the few people who asked me how I was doing. And I thought she came up to the department to see me…until I realized she was really coming up to see you." Victoria's mouth dropped. "Unless she was really there to see Wagner."

"I asked how you were doing a lot, too, you know," Jeff said, disregarding her other observations. "You always avoided eye contact with me, though. Hold on." Jeff took the sharp turn at full speed. The man knew more back roads than she thought existed. He glanced at her. "Why was that anyway? Why'd you never look me in the eye?"

The air in the cabin of the truck seemed to grow hot and stuffy. "There's something vulnerable about making eye contact for me. I didn't want to be attracted to you." She gasped. "Do you think Wagner was having an affair with April? And if so, maybe she was the one who shot him and set the house on fire!"

"Whoa." Jeff laughed. "I'm afraid I'm going to need a little more explanation. You didn't make eye contact because you were afraid you would become attracted to me? All this time, I thought you were scared of me or hated me."

"Does it really matter?" Victoria crossed her arms. "You were my supervisor back then, anyway. Back when we had jobs." She sighed. "I think we should focus on getting ourselves out of this mess. Why would April shoot Wagner, though?"

He took a deep breath. "Okay. Fine. April… Uh, I remember she told me she grew up in foster care. We've already established the car she drives. Yes, she might have been having an affair with Wagner, and they might have fudged the stock reports together. If so, she shot him because he was getting cold feet. If he'd remained conscious a little longer I genuinely think he would've talked."

"And if Wagner is still alive, he's in danger," Victoria concluded. "All the more reason to get our evidence as fast as we can."

Victoria opened the glove compartment to look for paper and a pen. She brainstormed best if she could make a list. "I wonder if she's done this before. I can't believe we both know the woman, and that's all we have to go on. Do you even know where she lives?"

"I don't know much anymore." He frowned. "Tell me again…you worked somewhere you thought this happened."

"Yes, but in that instance, it seemed I was wrong." Her hand flew to her mouth. "Wait. You think I wasn't?"

"Tell me about it."

"Pretty similar situation at Rancher Engineering. Except when I told them about it, they asked me to leave."

"Rancher Engineering." He tapped the steering wheel with each syllable. "Rancher Engineering. I know that name."

"It was a gigantic company, probably three or four times the size of Earth Generators. It was about to become a blue chip stock, so it was in the news for a while. Earth Generators is about to become a blue chip stock now, too." Victoria did her best to mimic the market watch announcers she'd heard on television. "It's up and coming, the one to watch."

"I…I think we better find out if April worked there, as well."

"You…you think I could've been right there, too?"

"You said it was a huge company. Did you know anyone in HR?"

"No." She slapped her hand on her knee. "If it turns out your hunch is right, this will be the second time that woman has tried to ruin my life."

Jeff held up a hand. "I was thinking aloud. We don't know that for sure."

She tapped her nails on the car armrest. "Think about it. April tried to get all the other ladies at work to think you were off-limits, so she could have you for herself. But you didn't take the bait. Maybe she wanted you to help her commit fraud, but she found out you valued your integrity too much, so she needed to go further up the food chain to Wagner. If Wagner had been having an affair with her, she would've found out everything she needed to know about our accounting procedures. And as soon as Wagner suspected I had found them out…" She gave Jeff a sideways glance. "April decided to take care of both of us."

"I don't see how this is helping. Even if we conclude she is behind it, there could be many more. Let's get the evidence and turn it over to as many people as possible. That seems the safest route."

As they drove in silence, the tension returned to her spent muscles. Her mind flooded with what-if questions. She leaned over and turned on the radio. The melodies helped soothe her wild emotions as the highway led them closer to hope, but her mind still ran a mile a minute.

She stared at Jeff's profile, the shadows crossing his

face as they passed other headlights. "Why did you work at Earth Generators if skydiving was what you really loved to do?"

"It paid the bills, and I've been saving away to start my own business."

"What business?"

"Someday I'd like to start an indoor skydiving business. Essentially, it's a wind tunnel so people can experience skydiving without as much risk. Tourists would eat it up. I'd still jump and eventually be able to teach and test for USPA certifications, but I wouldn't run very many tandem flights."

"And you'd do that with Drake?"

"My right-hand man." He nodded. He glanced her way. "You still worried about Baloo? Because I promise he's in good hands. And I gave Drake strict instructions not to contact me, so I don't think he's in any danger."

"Thank you," she responded but didn't stop looking at him when he turned his attention back to the road. Her question hadn't been based on worry for Baloo; she found herself wanting to know more and more about Jeff. All her preconceived risk analysis formulas concerning him had been proven wrong. She found herself in dangerous territory, not knowing how to guard her heart anymore.

The GPS informed them they were six-hundred feet from the DataCrypt offices. "Why are you slowing down?"

"April might be there or have already beaten us. This might be a trap."

Jeff pulled to the side of the road underneath several large oak trees. He pointed across the street at the row of houses. "A truck parked in the middle of nowhere is suspicious. Hopefully people will assume we're visiting one of these houses." He stepped out of the truck and walked around to meet her. "We need to cross this field and just past the grove of trees. If I'm right, we'll run right into DataCrypt's back lot."

"I guess that makes sense." The crisp, dark air heightened Victoria's senses. "If only we could use a flashlight or our cell phones."

Jeff reached out and took her hand. Victoria had a hard time focusing on anything when he touched her. She started to pull away until he said, "So we keep each other from falling."

"Or take each other down. I'm not sure I could hold you up if you trip."

He chuckled, but she couldn't see his face. "I was trying to not offend."

"Oh, so you think that you can't possibly fall, but I, a clumsy woman, will likely tank?"

Before he could issue a snarky comeback, they both tripped over something. Victoria instinctively let go of Jeff's hand to catch her fall. Her hands hit the hard dirt.

"I think I just proved a proverb." Jeff stood up and brushed off his pants, then reached a hand out toward her.

"Pride isn't usually followed so quickly with a fall." Victoria accepted his help to stand up. "What did we trip over?" She squinted to try to make out the long shape behind her.

"A log, I think."

A flash of light blinked through the trees ahead. "Jeff, look. What was that light?" A gust of wind blew against her skin, throwing her hair back, as the sky brightened. A cloud moved aside to let the moon's light show them the way.

Jeff's shadow pointed ahead to the path before them. "It might have been headlights. I can't tell. We need to hurry."

Victoria looked up to the sky and instantly spotted her favorite constellation. She whispered a prayer of thanks for the unhindered moonlight, then jogged to keep up with Jeff. He still held her hand, but his pace was so fast she worried she was about to leave her legs behind and get dragged the rest of the way. As if he could hear her thoughts, he released her hand and took the lead.

The moonlight revealed a tilled row prepped for planting season. "Try to keep up." Jeff jogged on the raised mound, and Victoria followed, making sure to leave enough room between the two of them. If Jeff tripped, she wanted enough space to stop before hitting him, and she certainly didn't want to fall into his broad back. At the grove of trees, Jeff stopped and raised a hand, indicating she should heed his example.

"Now would be a good time for the moon to disappear again," he whispered.

Victoria brazenly tiptoed in front of him, through a stand of trees, barely making a sound. Jeff followed, his feet causing all the layers of leaves below him to crackle. His sneaking skills needed some serious work. He might have speed on his side, but she had stealth.

At the last tree, a foot of thick manicured grass led to a curb behind a parking lot. "This must be it." She pointed to the back of the building. "I don't see any lights in the building. You were right. It must've been headlights I saw in the field."

Jeff took a step closer to her, his body mere inches from her back. Victoria could feel his warm breath on her neck but tried to disregard the closeness. She tried to convince herself it was merely the wind. They needed a plan of action. She tilted her head, so he could hear her better. "First, we try to get in with our Earth Generators badges—you have yours, right? Maybe we can use your IT friend's name and phone number as backup. He'll vouch for us, right?"

"I don't feel comfortable asking him to do that," he whispered.

His breathy whispers in her ear tickled. Victoria took a step to the right, her hand flying to the side of her face. "This is no longer just about us. Wagner's life, your aunt and uncle…people could die if we don't end this."

"I don't think we'll need to go that far. Garrett had some ideas for me to gain access."

She frowned. "How?"

His eyes widened. "Can we just focus on the present moment?"

"Okay, fine." She sighed, staring at the building's back door.

He pressed a hand on her back. "Let's go."

They walked across the parking lot purposefully until Victoria's stomach turned. "Stop!" She grabbed his arm. "Jeff, do you smell it?" The acrid smell of burned plastic assaulted her senses. Having the stuff in her lungs twice in two days, there was no mistaking the smell of arson.

"Now I do."

The back door of DataCrypt burst open, and an employee ran out of the building, coughing. Black smoke billowed behind him, disappearing into the dark night. "Are you okay?" she shouted, but didn't move forward.

"Stay here." Jeff ran up to the man. He nodded, coughing.

Jeff pointed inside. "Is there anyone else in there?"

Her heart squeezed. Jeff was ready to run inside, and if he did, she was going in with him. The guy shook his head. The sound of sirens filled the air. She closed her eyes. April had done this. She felt sick to her stomach. There was nothing they could do here. She almost called Jeff's name aloud, but her voice caught with emotion.

"He's okay—the only one on duty. Help is coming," Jeff said, jogging toward her. He grabbed her hand and guided her back through the trees. Victoria looked over her shoulder to find the employee staring after them.

"They'll think we started the fire," she said. "I almost said your name aloud!"

"Just run."

She let go of his hand as they hit the same channel of dirt. "Look for the log," she huffed, pumping her arms hard and fast. His long legs covered several feet at a time with each step.

"Jump!"

She saw him move before his word registered and instinctively leaped over the log like a hurdle. The channel disappeared into flat ground. They sprinted toward the truck just as the sirens grew louder.

They flung their doors open. Victoria looked over her shoulder and saw flashes of red and yellow through the trees. Jeff put the truck in motion before her seat belt was engaged. Victoria let her head fall into her hands and gulped for air. Her lungs burned, and her heart was sure to burst through the rib cage it pounded against.

"Lift your arms."

She sat up. "What?"

"Lift your arms. It'll help you catch your breath faster."

She obeyed and the pain eased. A moment later, her heart rate had almost returned back to normal. She dropped her shoulders. "I feel defeated. Utterly defeated. Can't anything go right?"

He squeezed the steering wheel tight. "They should be able to get the fire out fast."

Despair turned to rage. Her eyes burned, her throat burned. Where would they go now? "We need to call April and put a stop to this once and for all. Make sure you're recording the conversation. Talk to her and she might slip up, might give us enough to take to the police."

Jeff shook his head and sped through the subdivision. Where was he was going? "I doubt she'd be that gullible," he said. "Her impatience gave us an edge. If Garrett is right, she doesn't know yet there is a backup server at the office. We're going to have to beat her to it."

"We have no idea how to get into the office if our badges don't work. Please, make the call."

Jeff grunted but pulled over next to a neighborhood park, turned on his phone and punched in the number. "It went straight to voice mail."

"So, we try again later."

He smirked.

"Do you have a better idea?"

He shook his head and coughed. "Water."

She reached behind the seat for the insulated bag Aunt Katie had provided. Jeff put the truck back in gear. It was nearing eight o'clock. Before her life fell apart, she would've been enjoying a book and a hot bath by now. She found the water right next to something squishy, wrapped in tinfoil. Jeff accepted the water and guzzled it. She peeked in the tinfoil to find fudgy brownies.

She stiffened, her hand frozen in the air.

"What? What is it?"

She faced him. "The fudge. The fudge for the security guards." Her mind connected the dots. "I know what we have to do."

SIXTEEN

Jeff groaned. The situation proved difficult enough without one of them going loopy. "Victoria, what are you talking about?"

"I need a clear head." She placed both of her hands on the side of her head and closed her eyes. "Listen. Anytime I make dessert, I bring most of them in to share, right? I leave a lot for the security guards—Charlie and the other guys—remember?"

"Victoria—"

She shook her hands in front of her. "Don't you see? We need to talk to Charlie. Think about it. He's the only one we can trust from the company. Right? There's no way he'd believe you blew up your own car. He was there!"

Jeff mulled it over. It was so tempting to be able to talk to someone who could potentially give wisdom. They certainly weren't making any headway on their own.

"I'm sure he would help us," Victoria continued. "He can get us in the building."

"You'd be willing to risk his job?"

"Of course not! He could—I don't know—get us a blueprint of the building and *accidentally* leave it for us while going to get coffee or something."

"Yeah, you're dreaming."

She glared at him. "Okay, maybe he won't have blueprints of the corporate offices lying around, but that's not the point. We just need to think outside the box. Let's get someone to at least hear our story and check on Wagner in the hospital. If he's still alive, he could warn the authorities."

Jeff nodded. "Agreed on that count."

"Good. First step will be tracking down where he lives because I doubt he's in the yellow pages."

"I think I can help you with that."

Even in the dim light of the truck's cab, Jeff could tell Victoria was pouting. "I don't see why this is so upsetting to you."

"I'm not upset." She took a tentative taste of a brownie. "I just don't see why he invites you over for dinner when I've been making his family gourmet treats for the past three years."

"Maybe because you didn't help fulfill one of his son's dreams."

"Which was?"

"Skydiving."

She gave him a pointed look. "I take it you didn't almost get Charlie's son killed."

"Nice. Real nice. I think we've already established that our skydive wasn't the norm."

Victoria leaned back into the seat. "I know, but I either tease you or cry about it. Which do you prefer?"

"Tease away." He tapped a finger on the dashboard clock. "It's getting late. I hope he's not asleep already." Jeff turned the truck into a long private road leading to a California Mission two-story home lit up by large standing lanterns on either side of the driveway. Victoria gaped.

"Nice, huh?" Jeff smiled, enjoying the fact he'd visited before.

"How does a security officer own a home like this?"

Jeff shrugged. "I think his wife used to be a lawyer. She's retired but advises for charities. Charlie was in law enforcement," he muttered. He couldn't quite remember what branch.

Victoria placed a hand over her heart. "I think we qualify as needing charity right about now."

He cut the truck's engine and stared at the front door. "You sure you want to do this? Charlie might not believe us, and we might end up in jail sooner than later."

"Or, he could give us the help we desperately need." The truck wobbled slightly as a result of her knee bouncing rapidly in place. "I can't stop thinking that if I had let a ton of people in on this from the very beginning, then there wouldn't be any weight in the charges against us. Everything would've been diluted if I'd given up my fear of being wrong." Victoria turned to him, her blue eyes reflecting off the light from the lanterns. "If I'm honest with myself, I didn't want to give up my pride. I wanted to be the surest accountant in the world." Her shoulders slumped. "It was dumb. And now I think it's time to reach out and trust. If it's the wrong person, then hopefully God sends more help our way. I'm out of ideas, Jeff."

Jeff put a hand over hers and squeezed. "Let's go, then." Jeff held her shaking hand as they walked up the cobblestone pathway. He wondered if she was ready to reach out and trust him, as well. Victoria rang the doorbell. A moment later the door swung open to reveal a very different-looking Charlie than the security guard they saw every weekday. In a maroon long-sleeve shirt, dark jeans and brown slip-on loafers, Charlie looked to Jeff like a relaxed movie star.

"Well, hello," Charlie said, his rich-timbre voice as soothing as always. "I wondered if I'd be seeing you two."

Victoria gawked as Charlie stepped back and gestured for them to come in. She obeyed and marveled at the glittering glass chandelier in the foyer. She stepped onto the oriental runner on top of the gleaming hardwood floors.

Charlie closed the door, smiling. The man seemed to enjoy her astonishment. "You're not surprised to see us?" she asked.

He blinked slowly, his lips slightly downturned. "No, I suppose not. After our little interchange Friday morning, strange things started happening. Not the least being Jeff's car blowing up." He walked ahead of them down the hallway. "That was a shame." Charlie turned to the left and opened French glass doors to reveal a large, stately dining room. He waved his fingers. "Come. Sit. I'll get us something to drink."

The moment he was out of the room, she poked Jeff in the chest. "You ate here and didn't freak out that the security guard was actually loaded?"

"We didn't eat in here. They have a normal-looking kitchen table in the kitchen, and I parked and came in the back with his son."

Victoria pulled out an elegant wooden dining room chair. "Would you look at this wood? This is made out of teak, Jeff. Teak! It's the most expensive wood used in furniture." She let her fingers travel along the edge.

"Maybe he didn't want you to see the rich part reserved for his wife's clients."

A woman in her early sixties entered the room wearing a flowing red blouse, tan slacks and leather sandals. She glided to the dining room table with a tray of bottled waters and a bowl of popcorn. "Nice to see you again, Jeff. Perfect timing. We were just about to start movie night and had treats ready to go."

She placed the tray in the center of the table. Her red, jeweled necklace caught Victoria's eye. Possibly sensing her stare, the woman reached out for a handshake from Victoria. "I'm Charlie's wife, Christy. I'm glad to finally meet you. The fudge that came home Wednesday was delicious. I wish I could say I had some left but we had the kids over for lunch this weekend." She straightened. "I'd ask for the recipe, but I'm hopeless in the kitchen."

Charlie entered the room with his smartphone in hand. He sat down and placed his phone in the middle of the table.

"What exactly did happen with Jeff's car?" Victoria asked. "We saw you in the parking lot afterward. You weren't hurt, were you?"

"Nah." Charlie pointed to Jeff. "I saw a red Range Rover on the cams. Didn't even have the brains to park correctly. He just pulled up, kept the car running, did something to your car, and drove off. So I went to investigate."

Victoria gasped and squeezed Jeff's arm. "He saw the vehicle! Someone else saw the vehicle!" She spun back. "Did you tell the police?"

Charlie raised an eyebrow. "Did I tell the police? What kind of question is that, Miss Hayes?"

"I'm not trying to offend you. You can't possibly know

how relieved I am that someone else saw the guy who's been following me."

"Wasn't just me. We got it on camera." His fingers intertwined and rested atop the table.

She grabbed Jeff's arm and shook it in excitement. "Evidence."

Jeff placed a hand over Victoria's in an attempt to calm her, no doubt.

"Now, hold on," Charlie said. "This isn't some high-tech camera that could make out the license plate or even identify the perp. We can see it's the vehicle that matches the description coupled with my eyewitness report."

She sighed. "So, not much."

"Not much," he agreed.

Jeff leaned forward. "Charlie, what happened when it exploded?"

"I thank the good Lord and a bunch of acorns for keeping me safe. I was approaching your car when a strong wind blew. The oak trees lining the road let loose some big clumps of leaves complete with the nuts. They hit the roof of your car and…"

"Boom," Jeff finished.

He leveled a finger at Jeff. "Boom."

Victoria eyed the smartphone Charlie placed in the middle of the table and wondered if he had just called someone. "Why did you think we'd come here? All because my badge had been revoked?"

He turned his palms over. "I hear things. Security guards start to get viewed as furniture, and people say all manner of things without giving it a second thought. Bit by bit, I start getting an idea of what's going on in the company. For instance, I know that it wasn't a fluke that your badge doesn't work anymore, and it made me think you're in some sort of trouble."

Jeff reached for a bottle of water. "Well, you would be right. We are in trouble, and we need to get into the building to prove we're innocent before someone else gets there first."

Charlie's eyes examined each of their faces without his expression giving any indication of what he was thinking. Victoria had never been intimidated by Charlie until that moment.

He leaned back into his chair and smiled. "You want my help to get in?"

"We don't want to get you in trouble," Victoria said, hastily. "We're hoping there's a way you can help us without hurting the integrity of your job."

Charlie put a hand over his eyes and started laughing. "Well, that's a pretty tall order." He dropped his hand just enough to peek at them. "You hoping I accidentally leave my badge in the room and come back to find you gone?"

Victoria was hit by a wave of dizziness from the intense, sudden heat in her gut. If Jeff admitted that was, in fact, exactly what she was thinking, she'd slug him right in the shoulder. Worse, Charlie's mock idea was better than her blueprint one, as his badge had clearance for the entire building. She decided silence was the best answer to Charlie's question.

He leaned back into his chair, folded his hands and said, "Here's what I suggest. Tell me everything and let *me* decide what will and won't hurt the integrity of my job."

Charlie's wife stood and stepped out of the room. Victoria looked at Jeff to see if they were in agreement.

"I'm game," Jeff said. "He trusted me with his son, so I'm willing to trust him."

Charlie gave a slight nod in recognition. Christy re-entered the room holding a yellow legal pad and a ball-point pen, and took her seat.

"You…you want her to write it all down? Why? Because she's going to be our legal counsel?" Victoria looked back and forth between the husband and wife, trying to ascertain what was happening.

Christy didn't look up. Instead, she jotted down notes and focused on her legal pad. Charlie tilted his head slightly, his bottom lip sticking slightly out. He seemed to be studying both of them. A moment later he shrugged. "Sure."

Victoria glanced at Jeff. His eyes were wide, but he reached over, squeezed her hand and gave her a nod. Feeling bolstered by Jeff's approval, she took a deep breath and started to recite the whole sordid story. Charlie interjected occasionally to ask clarifying questions, but mostly she rattled out every detail she could remember. His wife's hand didn't stop scribbling until Victoria recounted Darcy texting her that April had said they were wanted in connection to shooting Wagner.

Christy glanced over her nose at Charlie, and they shared what seemed to be a meaningful glance. Victoria pressed on with their story until the time line brought them to Charlie's table.

The silence afterward felt deafening. Her leg twitched, ready to run. Charlie tapped the table. "So, the stakes are high, but April doesn't know about the office backup server."

Jeff's phone vibrated. "Sorry. I forgot to turn it off after we tried to confront April." He paled.

"What is it?" Victoria asked and leaned over to see his phone screen. It was a text from Garrett.

You said you were in trouble, not wanted by the police. Big difference, man! Not cool. I've let April know what we discussed. She's contacting the police. I like you, man, but if you just got me involved in something bad, I'll come after you myself.

Victoria cringed. "April knows about the backup server now. We're running out of time, Charlie. Can you help us or not?"

"I had hoped with all the connections with the other security guards that you might be able to put us in touch with some authorities that could go with us to retrieve the evidence," Jeff added.

Charlie turned away and nodded at Christy. She stood up and walked to the swinging door as Charlie rose and placed his hands on the table and leaned forward. "I do have some connections, but that's going to take some time to set up—I'm guessing close to an hour. Time," he said, "you don't have. Either way, I need to make some phone calls and report you stopped by my house for a few minutes. I'm sorry we couldn't be of more assistance." He pushed off from the table, straightened and exited the dining room with Christy by his side.

Victoria wanted to cry. He was reporting them.

"Victoria," Jeff said softly. "Let's hurry." Jeff stood and reached across the table.

She looked up in time to see a security badge resting in the very place Charlie's hand had pressed into the table a few seconds prior.

"Sounds like we have less than an hour before authorities join us." He reached out for her hand, and they ran out the door. "Remember the text you got at my uncle's? They wanted us back at the office. This might be a trap."

"I know, but it's our only hope...and maybe Wagner's only hope, too."

SEVENTEEN

Jeff did his best to stay on back roads from the moment he left Charlie's house until he neared their workplace. It took a great effort to restrain his foot from slamming on the gas.

He parked in the shadows beside the evergreens guarding the closest subdivision entrance. Victoria unbuckled her seat belt and bolted out of the truck before him. He rushed to catch up to her before she crossed the street onto company property. "Victoria, wait, please."

She tilted her face and stared unabashedly into his eyes. The streetlights, the moon and the stars…they all seemed to emphasize the beauty standing before him. He remembered the reason she'd said she never wanted to look him in the eye. He thought it was a ridiculous notion until now when his heart strained against his chest. "I'm starting to be glad you never looked me in the eye before this week."

She cocked her head to the side and put her hands on her hips. "This is our only hope and you wanted me to wait for that?"

He shook his head. "No, no. It came out all wrong. I…I wanted you to know I'm not your supervisor."

She raised an eyebrow. "I know…we don't have jobs anymore."

"No." He looked up into the cloudless night. If he could abort, he would, but it was too late now. *Lord, a little help. My tongue seems to be tied.* He blew out a breath. "Friday was supposed to be my last day as supervisor. Wagner had set the wheels in motion for me to be transferred to a different department." Jeff raked a hand through his hair. "I realize now it was likely motivated by whatever scheme he had concocted with April, but I wanted you to know."

"Why?" Her voice was soft. "Why are you telling me now? Why didn't you tell me when I showed up at your apartment?"

"Because you were already so upset and I didn't want you to…"

Her eyes narrowed. "You didn't want me to feel guilty that I had come to you for help."

"Yes, and later, I was afraid if I told you the truth, after our kiss, you'd see it as a player move." He took a deep breath. "But I want it all out before we go in there. In case it's our last moment of freedom. Victoria, you said it would never work because I've been waiting for the perfect woman. But you were wrong."

Her eyes widened.

"I wasn't waiting for some elusive perfect woman. What I was waiting for was the perfect woman for me."

She smiled the smallest of smiles.

"Someone smart, warm, funny, kind and willing to fight for what is right no matter the cost. Victoria, you are—"

She wrapped her arms around his neck and kissed him fiercely. Then just as quickly, she broke off the embrace and took a step back, her eyes vibrant. She wiped a tear off her cheek, then pulled her shoulders back and flashed a flirtatious smile. "Now that you're officially not my boss, I can call the shots, too, right? Let's go earn our freedom, Jeff." She winked, then ran across the street into the night.

The back of the Earth Generators, Inc. corporate offices looked like a bunker compared to the inviting front entrance. All Victoria could see was concrete and small slits of office windows. One large metal door with ridges, presumably for truck loading, and a smaller metal door ten feet to the right seemed to be the only entry points.

Victoria looked over her shoulder to find a stunned Jeff running after her. She wanted to take time to dwell on the kiss and his proclamation, but it was the very thing pushing her to speed up. She had lived her whole adult life by the book. She had finally found love; she was not about to be framed without a fight.

Jeff caught up, and they walked the remainder of the perimeter together. In the truck, Jeff had told her they needed to act as if they belonged there, so Victoria silently chanted it to herself. "We belong here. We belong here."

Jeff clutched her hand, indicating they stop at the corner. They leaned against the wall of the building, several feet away from a security camera.

Victoria pointed ahead of them. "Have you ever been through this door?"

Jeff shook his head. "Security is one department I've never worked in."

"This should be in and out. We'll be fine. In and out."

He looked right into her eyes. "Who are you trying to convince? You or me?"

Victoria straightened. She didn't want to explain that she was giving herself a pep talk. "I wish we could've found some wigs and security guard uniforms first. I was a little surprised Charlie didn't have some disguise for us to borrow. I mean, at the very least you could've worn his uniform jacket."

Jeff's mouth dropped open. "You just told me you were worried we were going to get him into trouble, and now you wish he would've handed over more than his badge?"

Her cheeks heated. "I'm a complicated woman."

He looked into her eyes again and smiled. "I won't argue with that."

Victoria instinctively smiled back until his words registered. "Hey!"

He grinned and gave her a gentle nudge toward the door. "We can discuss my faux pas later, Victoria. Let's live in the present moment."

She froze as she reached for the handle. "No worries," she whispered.

Jeff held up Charlie's badge to the proximity scanner. The lock unclicked, and Victoria pressed on the handle. The door swung open. She stepped in, looked down at the floor and made a quick side step to the right. Jeff repeated her actions one step behind her. She glanced up and immediately spotted the video camera on the far corner. Just as Charlie had described.

She slid along the wall. Half lockers were opposite her. Her feet seemed paralyzed. "I'm so nervous," she whispered.

Jeff leaned over her shoulder and, in a whisper, said,

"You're not a thief. You're trying to prevent a thief. You're a…a spy, really. Maybe informant is a better word."

Victoria wondered if Jeff had figured out her habit of self-pep-talks and was trying to reinforce her courage. Instead his attempt made her want to laugh. She examined the ceiling; they were directly underneath another camera. "Give me the badge, Jeff." She smiled shyly when his hand touched hers.

Victoria flicked the badge up to the black reflective square next to the door and heard the telltale click of the door unlocking. She did her best to mold herself to the door frame as she slipped into the adjoining hallway.

Jeff straightened and simply walked behind her. No creeping, no sliding. Victoria gaped at him. "What if the security camera had caught you?"

"Then they probably would think I was a normal person. If they saw someone sneaking, then wouldn't that cause suspicion? Besides, we're inside now and it's—" he pulled out his smartphone "—after ten o'clock. I don't think anyone will be watching the security guard locker room very closely. And there is no camera in this hallway."

She looked down the nondescript beige carpet to the left and right. "Charlie said go right to the elevator?"

"Yep."

The adrenaline rushed through her veins. Her step and stride grew longer as her mind rehearsed the plan. They strode into the arriving elevator, pressed the fifth-floor button, and the doors closed. "And now they will be able to see us," she said. "There's no way around it."

"Yes, but how likely is it that anyone of consequence will?" Jeff put a hand on her shoulder. "If anyone sees us, they won't know that our access has been denied. In fact, they'll most likely recognize us as employees and not give it another thought."

"Unless, like I reminded Charlie, April and her co-horts have already put them on alert. They've been one step ahead of us this entire time. Why should I think any different?" The elevator door slid open. "Showtime." Victoria grinned at Jeff. "I've always wanted to say that."

They walked into an open room filled with cubicles and large open offices against the wall. It was an exact replica of every other working floor in the building. The realization was a little disappointing, really. In her mind, the IT department would look much more high-tech with gigantic touch-screen monitors hung from the ceiling while colorful graphics indicated everything that was going on in the network in real time. Instead, it looked exactly like her accounting department.

She hoped Jeff was right about no one of consequence caring about their presence because the video cameras were set up in every corner of the large cubicle farm. It was probably the only difference between this floor and the rest. More security. They were out in the open, and she felt like a walking target.

She continued to the center of the room, then spun around in a circle. "Now, where is it?"

Jeff mimicked her moves.

"There." She pointed to what looked like another carpeted wall panel, the exact same gray fabric as the rest of the cubicle walls, except there was a metal ring handle embedded into the panel at waist level. More importantly, a paper sign was stapled to the panel: "This is not the room you are looking for."

Jeff smirked. "You can't have an IT department without some humor."

She strode to the panel, lifted the handle, turned it and opened the door. She heard the machines before she could see them. It sounded like a wind turbine rotating in a room the size of a double-length walk-in closet. She stepped up into the enclosure. Tall towers filled with racks and racks of computer equipment lined the ten-foot enclosure. All black-and-silver equipment, this was the impressive show of technology Victoria had been expecting. She reached her hand out toward a machine but stopped before touching. "I feel like I'm looking at a library of technology instead of books."

"That's because you are."

A large high-pitched sound erupted throughout the room, causing her to jump.

Jeff put both hands on her shoulders. "It's okay. It's just the humidifier kicking in. They have to keep this room between 40 and 60 percent humidity. This desert air could cause static electricity."

She looked down and found they were standing on massive grates lining the room.

"For air conditioning," Jeff said. "This is the most important room in the building."

She eyed him. "How do you know all this?"

"Garret gave me quite the education on server rooms. He wanted to make sure I knew how to access the tapes." He stepped to her right and pointed at one rack that looked remarkably similar to a tape deck player. In it sat a tape that looked the width of a cassette tape but the thickness of the old beta tapes back in the days of VHS. "And I'm glad he did. Otherwise, I'd never have recognized this as what we're looking for. Here you go."

"Yes!" She groaned and stomped her foot on the grate. "It has this week's date on it." She spun around and knelt in front of a small metal cabinet filled with shelves. "Wait. There are more dates. Look." Victoria handed him a blue tape with the date a few weeks back when she'd filed the original reports. "It's got to be on this one."

Jeff fingered the tape and stared at the rack of shelves. "Now the trick is how to access it." He pressed the eject symbol next to one of the drives, and the current tape popped out. Once he replaced it, he heard an even louder whirring through the machines. "Garrett said there would be a laptop, but I don't see one anywhere."

Victoria tentatively reached her hands out. "My brother says that everything IT-related is hidden, or at least not obvious. Just like this server room. You have to know what you're looking for." She carefully ran her fingertips down the large tower of racks until she stopped at one black rectangle with three raised horizontal lines at the top, right in the center. She glanced at Jeff, nervous, and pushed the three raised lines.

Her hands jerked backward in alarm as a tray popped out toward her. She stared down at a very large laptop and lifted the monitor.

"Okay, so that was very cool." Jeff took his place in front of the laptop while Victoria stood by the door to play lookout.

EIGHTEEN

Jeff typed in Bill's username and prayed for it to work. His phone buzzed. He glanced down at his pocket—the temptation to ignore it strong—but the realization that it could be Charlie won out. He quickly slipped it out of his pocket. It was April. Should he answer to lead her off the trail? Victoria was too far away to get her attention. "Hello?"

"It's helpful to know where all the camera blind spots are, isn't it? I know it's come in handy many times for myself."

Jeff gazed at the security camera in the corner, instantly recognizing the voice. "That's interesting, April. Why don't you tell me about all those times?" He angled his body so the camera couldn't see his left hand as he began typing in Bill's password.

"My friend is pointing a gun at your girlfriend, so I suggest you shut up and stop typing. Take the tape out of the deck."

Jeff exhaled and closed his eyes. So close, yet so far. He glanced to his left and saw Victoria's side at the entrance of the server room, her face pointed to a far corner of the room, her body stiff and unmoving. She must've seen the gunman. He clicked the phone on speaker and dropped it in his pocket.

Jeff moved to the tape deck and removed the tape in question.

"Take it over to the machine next to the door." April's voice was cold and firm.

Jeff turned, his back now to the camera, and walked slowly with the tape, looking to the left and right for any weapon or shield that might help them. Nothing. Only extra tapes.

"Insert the tape into the machine."

Jeff stood in front of the machine labeled Degauss Data Eliminator.

"Wouldn't this have been easier than torching Data-Crypt?" he asked, looking up at the camera. He needed to keep her focused on his face for just another second.

"Oh, please. That was fun. Especially seeing you two run. Besides, it was before your friend Garrett gave me an education on backup tapes. Seems all we have to do is demagnetize them. Step to the side and let me see you put in the tape."

He obeyed and inserted the tape into the machine and pressed a button labeled Degauss. The machine began clicking.

"Thank you. Not nearly as satisfying as a fire, though. Turn and please stare right into the security camera."

Jeff wasn't a violent man, but he really hated being toyed with, and he would have liked nothing more than to break the camera. Instead, he squeezed his phone as tight as possible.

"Oh, that's good. The anger is very evident. Now we have it on tape that I tried to reason with you. So the security guard aiming the gun at Victoria will seem perfectly reasonable. Goodbye, Jeff."

The phone rewarded his silence with a dial tone. Jeff ran for the door and raised both his arms, hoping that there was a real security guard on site, watching. "We surrender!" He caught sight of the gunman in the corner, underneath the security camera, pointing his weapon at Victoria. So, the guard didn't want to be caught on tape. Interesting. Jeff kept his arms raised and stepped to the side and then in front of her.

"It's him," she whispered. "The red cap guy."

"Put your arms down, you idiot!" The security guard shook his gun at him. "I don't have plans of killing you as long as you're not stupid. The cops are on their way."

Jeff stared at the man in the shadows. "I don't think that's a gun," he whispered.

"What do you mean?" she whispered.

"Looks more like a Taser, to me."

"Stop talking," the security guard shouted.

"A police Taser can shoot like thirty-five feet," Victoria said, not heeding the guard's warning, likely because the guard couldn't see her mouth behind Jeff's shoulder. He wanted to ask her how she knew that, but if he did, the guard would see his mouth move. "We might be past that," she continued, "but just barely. And if either of us is wrong, we get shot."

Jeff said nothing but slowly nodded.

The elevator dinged. The security guard tensed, holding his weapon. Appearing around the corner was another security guard. "Lloyd! What's going on here? You're not supposed to be on duty now."

"Police are coming," the gunman replied. "I've got this. You can go back down."

"Police? What'd these guys do?"

"They've been snooping around and stealing stuff."

Victoria peeked her head around Jeff. "It was just a misunderstanding," she hollered. "We work here. We have badges. He won't let us explain."

"I said, shut up!" the gunman yelled.

"Come on, Lloyd. They're unarmed. Put that away. I recognize that guy. He's a supervisor. I'm telling you, they're not going anywhere."

Lloyd turned on the guard. They heard a simultaneous electric sizzle and the other guard's scream as he collapsed to the ground.

Victoria didn't have time to react. Jeff yanked her wrist and pulled her around the corner, into the hallway. She scanned her head left and right for somewhere to hide, but Jeff flung them into the doorway to the left.

The lights in the stairway flickered on as they ran down as fast as her legs could take them. Jeff took two stairs at a time, but she could jump three steps to the landing before each turn. Her hand burned as it slid along the metal banister, but she refused to let go.

Lloyd's footsteps slapped on the concrete above them. "They're going down," Lloyd yelled. Who was he yelling at?

Jeff pushed open the second-floor door as he simultaneously grabbed her wrist. She sprinted after him, down the hallway, as fluorescent lights flickered on behind them. They rounded a corner into another hallway. She heard the door to the stairs slam. That meant Lloyd knew what floor they were on, and the motion sensors in the building would turn lights on in every room they entered.

As they passed an open room of cubicles, Jeff grabbed

a stapler and flung it across the room, causing lights to flicker on, all along its path.

Her lungs burned as they continued down the hallway and around the corner. Jeff halted and carefully opened a door. Victoria followed him inside and watched him gently allow the door to close.

"What was that?" she panted. "Where are we?"

He shook his head and started down another flight of stairs. "Wanted to get him on the wrong track so we could take another stairway." He breathed heavy. "No cameras in the stairways. Just at exits."

Victoria held her chest, as if trying to hold her pumping heart within, when they reached the first-floor level. They pressed their backs against the opposite wall of the emergency exit, where a solitary camera was aimed at the door.

"Not much farther," Jeff promised. He grabbed her hand and led her to the very next door. They slipped in, and lights instantly flipped on. "Stupid motion sensors."

Victoria took big gulps of air while scanning the room. Tiny shelves covered the walls. In the middle of the room, equipment she didn't recognize sat atop a long monstrous countertop.

"Mail room," Jeff explained, his breathing almost back to normal. He walked around the counter. "Sit on the floor and stay still. Text Charlie and tell him to call the police. Tell him which room we're hiding in. He'll have an easier time getting someone here fast than we will."

She gladly obeyed while he grabbed a chair. He jumped up on it and taped a piece of paper over the motion sensor. He hopped down and joined her on the floor. Within thirty seconds—that felt more like five minutes—they were sitting in the dark.

He sighed. "I don't think they'll look in here."

"But if they check the security cameras—"

"I was watching," he said, and gave her hand a squeeze. "I made sure we were running in the opposite corner of the cameras. If they caught us, they just got a little blip. How did you know about the Taser anyway?"

"I take a self-defense class once a year, and they sell them. But pepper spray is cheaper," she answered. "Jeff," she whispered. "I think I'm ready. I'm ready to give up and just pray that the truth will win."

"I'm ready, too, but only when the police show up," Jeff added. "My number-one priority right now is keeping you safe, and I can't guarantee that with April or that rogue guard." He dropped her hand, but she could sense he was turning toward her.

She twisted to face him. Although she couldn't see his face, she felt his breath on her forehead. "I think no matter what happens I'll be fine," she said. "We'll be fine. I've been putting all my trust in risk analysis instead of the Lord." She leaned back into the counter. "You think they let prisoners write to each other?" she asked, meaning it to be a joke, but Jeff stayed silent.

"Speaking of risks," he finally said, "this probably isn't the right time, but you didn't let me finish back there."

Victoria stiffened. His tone sounded so serious. Had she misread him once again?

"I wanted you to know that when I kissed you in the mountains…well, I know you thought it was the heat of the moment, but it wasn't spontaneous for me."

"You said I was the one who kissed you, anyway." She was so thankful the darkness hid her face.

He chuckled. "That may be true, but you beat me by

only half a second." He lowered his voice. "I need you to know I'm not the type of guy who goes around kissing girls indiscriminately."

"And I don't go around kissing guys that way either," she added, thinking of the two times she hadn't seemed able to help herself. "For the record, the second time was due to the time crunch. Don't expect me to go kissing you again."

He laughed. "Fair enough."

All this time, she'd thought of him as a ladies' man. In reality, it turned out he was the opposite. It seemed clear to her now, but if she was honest with herself, fear had blinded her to the truth. In fact, no matter how much she'd proclaimed her love of Jesus and analyzed risks, she had still chosen to live in fear. It seemed ironic that in the scariest situation of her life she had more peace now than in her day-to-day living.

His fingers touched her hand. "Victoria, are you okay?"

"You got us in the dark, but you know they'll eventually find us in here."

"Yes, but it'll take that Lloyd guy a while to figure that out."

"It won't take me nearly as long," a cold voice said as light from the hallway spilled over the counter they hid behind.

Jeff and Victoria stood up to find April pointing a gun directly at them, her left hand supporting the right, arms extended. Knowing this was no Taser, Victoria believed without a doubt April must've been their shooter in the foothills. And since there was no remorse on her face, April would have no problem shooting them.

"Aren't you worried they'll want to check your gun

against the bullet that shot Wagner?" Jeff asked. "Or how about the ones in my truck?"

Uncertainty flickered over April's forehead. "They have no reason to suspect anything from me. I was here preparing my two weeks' notice and saw the need to help out the security guard until the police could arrest two embezzlers."

"What about the bombs and the fire?" Victoria asked, seething.

"My partner hates guns. Bombs and fire are more his style. He can't hit the broadside of a barn if he tried. I, however, am an excellent shot. I don't know how you escaped unscathed last time, Victoria. I thought for sure I'd hit you. I won't miss next time, so don't try me." She blinked slowly. "And the police, I'm afraid, will find traces of the same ingredients used for your bombs and fires in Jeff's office."

"I understand why you're after me, but you didn't have to involve Jeff."

She batted her eyes. "Well, don't we think highly of ourselves?" She laughed. "Jeff was always part of the backup plan should someone start suspecting us. We needed a supervisor, to be believable. Too bad Wagner got cold feet. He was fun." She waved a hand away. "Ah, well, men truly are the weaker sex."

"I can't believe I ever thought you were my friend."

April faked a pout. "So sad. If you behave, you don't have to die, though. I have different plans for Wagner once he gets out of ICU. He's going to get a poisonous visit from his wife." She held her left fingers up in air quotes. "In fact, consider that my going-away present to you, Victoria. As your friend, I won't kill you.

"Now, Lloyd is on his way with a little present. All

you have to do is put your fingerprints on a few things. Then I'll make a little call to the police that we caught you trying to plant a bomb in here, and I can let you rot in jail while I move on to bigger and better things. Piece of cake, right? And I have no worries, as you two have no reason to be believed about anything." She winked at Jeff. "That pesky little thing called evidence."

Victoria's eyes darted to Jeff.

"Oh, sweetie. I guess you don't know," April said, her voice oozing with fake empathy. "He destroyed the evidence for me."

Jeff kept his eyes on April.

"You did what?" Victoria stared hard at Jeff, but something caught her peripheral vision. A few inches within one of the built-in mail room shelves under the counter, a letter opener glinted. She took a step closer to Jeff. Acting as if she was angry, she shoved him sideways a bit, causing him to sidestep. Now they both stood behind the large scanner. The movement gave her enough cover to grab the letter opener and hold it below, at her side.

Jeff glanced down at her, recognition in his eyes. "April made me do it," he said sternly. "So don't start blaming me for something I had no part of!" His hand yanked the scanner's cord out of the outlet at the same time as his outburst.

"Oh, like I'm supposed to believe that when you two have a dating history?"

"She asked me out once! Once! And I never called her back!" In a burst of pretend anger, Jeff shoved the scanner toward April.

"Hey!" April let out an outraged shout as the machine almost hit her feet. She jumped back just in time, lost her balance and shot the ceiling just above Jeff.

Victoria lifted her leg up and slid over the counter, letter opener raised and hit April's wrist with the butt of the knife. April screamed, and the gun dropped. Jeff joined her in time to kick the weapon across the room. Men in blue jackets ran down the hall, guns drawn.

"FBI!"

April screamed. "Help me! I've been trying to keep them back, but he's got a gun! He just dropped it!" She pointed at the floor where her weapon had been kicked. The agents pointed their guns at Jeff. One man pointed his gun at Victoria. "Lower the knife!"

"That's not true." Victoria made a show of lowering the letter opener to the ground in slow motion, then held up her hands and stood. She caught sight of Jeff, his face white. "April is the only one with fingerprints on the gun," she said to Jeff, loud enough for the agents to hear. "You just kicked it away. And I think that gun will match the bullet that shot Todd Wagner."

"You heard the lady," Charlie bellowed, and walked up through the middle of the agents. "These two are with me," he said, pointing at Jeff and Victoria. "Take Miss April Sherman in for questioning."

"Charlie?" Jeff asked, his eyes wide.

"There's another man. A security guard," Victoria blurted. "He's the one who set my house on fire, made the bombs and hurt another guard."

"April had a hand in all of it every step of the way. The guard's name is Lloyd," Jeff said. "If that's his real name. April let it slip they're partners."

Charlie turned to one agent and spoke to him in hushed tones. The agent nodded to another, and the pair jogged away, down the hallway.

The tallest agent instructed them to all leave the mailroom, leave the weapons untouched and step into the hallway. As they did so, Jeff put his arm around Victoria. She responded to his touch by hugging him back until something sharp hit her ribs. "Ouch!"

The agent pointed his weapon at them. "No touching."

"What is that?" Victoria asked Jeff.

Jeff held his hands up. "Officer, there is some evidence in my shirt."

Victoria put both hands to her mouth, her eyes teary. "Please, don't get my hopes up," she whispered.

The officer approached and pulled out a hard blue-cased tape from Jeff's shirt.

Victoria laughed, half crying at the sight of the date on the tape. "There's evidence on there that will prove the company, or at least April, was involved in corporate fraud."

Charlie took the tape from the agent. "More likely white-collar crime, Victoria. All those fake companies you found out about? April here created fake employees and companies so she could issue large checks to them as contractors. Once you started suspecting something, she made the HR reports look like she fired the contractors. And I suspect she's done this before and planned to do this again."

"Not only that, I expect she made a large profit knowing how the stocks would rise." Victoria narrowed her eyes at April. "Check Rancher Engineering. I used to work there and suspected something similar happening during my employment."

Jeff stared at Charlie. "How did you get the FBI to come so quickly?"

Charlie shrugged. "Well, you don't think I've always been just a security guard, do you?"

"You used to be FBI?" Victoria said, mouth agape.

"Retired," he said with a nod. "But I'm not above stepping in now and then. Keeps me young." Looking at Victoria's outraged face, he laughed. "You never asked!"

Charlie turned around to address the other agents.

The moment the Feds switched their attention away from them, Jeff wanted to resume the hug Victoria had started before getting interrupted. "Victoria, job or no job, I won't be your supervisor anymore. Would you go out on a second date with me?"

She frowned. "I was unaware we had ever gone on a first date."

He shrugged. "I thought given, uh…my reputation, we could skip the first one. As of today, the *Jeff Tucker Dinner Club* has been officially dissolved." He stole a quick glance at the agent who was still eyeing him. "I never want you to be able to say you were a member."

She looked as if she was fighting a smile as she nodded. "That's a pretty good reason." She met his gaze. "Yes, I'll go with you on a second date, Jeff."

It was all the encouragement he needed. Jeff pulled Victoria to him, and her eyes widened. "They said no touching."

He grinned. "I'm pretty sure they won't mind. I'm only expressing my gratitude for you saving the day."

She raised an eyebrow. "I thought it was you who saved the day."

He leaned down closer until his lips were a mere inch away from hers. "Well, then, I guess we have each other to thank."

She smiled and closed her eyes as he kissed her tenderly.

"Hey! I said no touching!"

Jeff released her and held his hands up but didn't step away.

Her beautiful eyes stayed locked on his.

"You're not even supposed to be talking to each other," the agent barked.

Behind him, Jeff heard Charlie laughing. "Give the lovebirds a break, Bob. We both know they're innocent. You won't be sorry, either. I'm telling you, she makes the most delicious fudge you've ever tasted."

NINETEEN

Her ears roared with the sound of wind rushing past her, into the plane. Her stomach clenched. No one was harnessed to her this time; it was up to her to make the first move.

Jeff stood on her right side at the plane's door while Hector stood on the other. While they weren't attached, they both had a firm grip of her harness on either side. She closed her eyes and whispered a prayer, then looked at Jeff and nodded. *One, two, three...fall!*

She closed her eyes for half a second and tried to block out the thought that she was about to hit speeds at over one-hundred-and-ten miles per hour. Skydiving school had its cons—namely, Victoria now knew more about the risks than ever before. Free-falling with Jeff and Hector holding her harness on either side, she focused on the landscape below.

It was easier to enjoy beauty now that April and Lloyd sat in jail. Wagner was on bail but awaiting a trial for aiding and abetting. Victoria had spent the past few months able to sleep in her own new home with Baloo by her side. Although Baloo enjoyed weekly visits from Katie and Dean to "pet sit" while she went diving with Jeff—

followed by long evenings out on the town. And Jeff often took Baloo to Aunt Katie's place while Victoria went to her Certified Fraud Examiners prep course.

A mere week after they'd returned to work, Jeff asked her to consider trying skydiving again. He'd insisted she give him another chance, now that no one wanted them dead or in jail. Victoria had agreed and found that she loved it. She'd never forget his look of pleased surprise when she'd suggested she continue training with him.

Now Victoria smiled as the wind caressed her face. She was pretty sure Jeff had figured out that she was no longer diving just to be with him. She had grown to love the sport as her own. It was exhilarating and fun, and Victoria loved being able to talk about his dream of opening a wind tunnel with proper terminology.

Besides that, today was a celebration. Just yesterday, she'd passed her last auditing test with flying colors and become a Certified Fraud Examiner. Thanks to Charlie's encouragement and a few of his connections, Victoria had jobs lined up as a consultant to the FBI. She'd never imagined God would give her the childhood dream of working with the FBI without having to live the life of an agent.

The nightly dinners the past few months with Jeff had been the highlights of her days, though. Especially since Jeff was no longer her supervisor. While she missed seeing his face pass her cubicle every day, it was a move Victoria respected.

After such an intense adventure together, she wondered if the connection—the attraction between them—would dull. Instead, it only increased. She'd helped him make a business plan and started diving with him. Life was good.

Jeff tapped her wrist and moved his hand to her arm as she made three practice touches to the pull cord. He beamed at her. At least she assumed he was beaming, because the wind exaggerated his features. Victoria smiled back and looked at the little lines on the ground to spy the designated landing area.

Five thousand feet. She waved Jeff and Hector away and pulled the cord. The parachute flung out and behind her at half speed. She lifted her hands up and grabbed the toggles that enabled the parachute to open in full flight. Peace. She imagined this was what it would feel like to truly soar like the eagles. The verse came to mind. What a beautiful illustration; no one could feel weary flying like this. Did eagles feel as if they were floating, suspended by air?

Two thousand feet. She pulled on both toggles at the same time to practice flaring the parachute. If she failed, her chute wouldn't have enough lift and would stall. Her heart rate increased. She was on her own now. Her eyes widened at the very thought. But she wasn't really, was she? That peace came from God. The same God who promised she was worth something, no matter what she did or didn't do at work, no matter what her parents or Jeff or anyone else thought. She could rest in that. The ground was closer now. She could see Jeff hundreds of feet ahead of her. He had already landed and was unclipping his harness. She was one hundred feet away. *Toggles up!*

The parachute flared, and her feet gently touched the ground. She remained standing as the strings and parachute fell behind her. She had done it.

"Yes!" Jeff jogged up to her. "You are a natural!"

Victoria smiled. "I had the best trainer."

She unclipped the harness, releasing her hold from the chute. Jeff took a step backward and unzipped his jumpsuit. Underneath the blue, Jeff wore a black suit, a sleek silver dress shirt and an azure tie. Victoria's breath caught. The man was gorgeous.

He smiled, bent down on one knee, slid his hand into his breast pocket and looked up.

"Jeff—

Jeff opened the black box to reveal a silver band with a sparkling princess-cut diamond in the center. "Victoria Hayes, you are worth more than rubies, you are more precious than all jewels."

Victoria placed her hand on her heart. She recognized what he was saying. He was quoting scripture to her?

"You've captured my heart, utterly and completely." His voice shook with emotion. "Will you go on a forever adventure with me and be my wife?"

She laughed, tears blurring her vision. "Yes," she whispered, nodding. "Yes," she said again, firmly.

He stood up and placed the ring on her finger. Victoria closed her eyes and let him kiss her, a sweet soft kiss with the hint of promise. She opened her eyes, and he took the smallest of steps backward. "I love you."

"I love you," she declared. She tilted her head. "Did Aunt Katie and Uncle Dean know you were asking me today?"

Jeff grinned, nodding. "Know? When I picked you up today, Aunt Katie let me sneak a peek on what she's been crocheting. Are you ready for this? It's a giant tuxedo dog sweater."

Victoria shook her head and laughed. "Poor Baloo. Being loved by two women so much is rough."

"Oh, believe me, I know. It's such a hardship." He

kissed her. "Are you ready to go?" He turned, his hands open, and invited her to take them.

She accepted and knew, without a doubt, Jeff was worth the risk.

* * * * *

Dear Reader,

Thank you for reading my first Love Inspired Suspense story. Every time I heard about scandals that resulted in hardworking, responsible adults losing their pensions, I wanted justice. It made me wonder what it would be like for teenagers to watch their parents lose everything. Would they grow up wanting to be in a position to prevent that from happening to anyone else? Or would they be scared to take risks? Or both? Victoria was the culmination of my questions, and what a journey she had to sort it all out!

Jeff and Victoria both triggered unresolved issues in their own lives. Somctimes I wonder if God allows that to happen in my life for my benefit, so I can grow and move forward. How about you? Most of all, their story reminds me to seize the day. And I hope the same for you!

Feel free to stay in touch at my blog:

www.writingheather.com

Blessings,

Heather Woodhaven

Questions for Discussion

1. Victoria's childhood dreams involved careers fighting injustice—filled with danger and adventure—until a series of painful events changed her path. What were your dreams?

2. What are your dreams now? How have they changed and why?

3. Jeff didn't realize he had a fear of abandonment until Victoria presented his behaviors in a big-picture format (the Jeff Tucker Dinner Club). Have you ever experienced big-picture realizations about your own behavior? How did that realization come about?

4. Victoria carries pepper spray and takes an annual self-defense class. Do you think her caution is reasonable or over the top? What measures do you take to feel safe?

5. Jeff's stress outlet was skydiving; Victoria's was walking in nature while letting her imagination run wild. What's yours?

6. Some cultures view eye contact as a sign of respect. Victoria sees it as a sign of vulnerability and trust—almost as if the eyes truly are the windows to the soul. What's your view?

7. Victoria thought she could analyze a person from afar and decide if they were high-risk or low-risk.

Since body language makes up at least half of communication, many people assume they know what someone is thinking based on their facial expressions or actions. Can you relate? Victoria realized such judgments were prideful and a deeper sign of worry. What do you think?

8. What is the difference between taking risks and taking a leap of faith?

9. In my own life, there have been times where I've been called to put a dream or goal down...only for God to ask me to pick it up again later. Only, the dream has been tweaked and changed, as if God was just waiting for me to be moldable enough to follow His will for His glory. Has this ever happened to you? Discuss.

COMING NEXT MONTH FROM
Love Inspired® Suspense

Available February 3, 2015

TO SAVE HER CHILD
Alaskan Search and Rescue • by Margaret Daley
When Ella Jackson's son goes missing, she'll stop at nothing
to bring him home. She turns to a brooding former soldier
to help track down the kidnapper before Ella is the next
to disappear.

FUGITIVE TRACKDOWN
Bounty Hunters • by Sandra Robbins
Bounty hunter Adam Knight doesn't hesitate when his
sister's best friend needs his help. The man who murdered
Claire Walker's father wants her dead...and Adam is her
only hope for survival.

TAKEN • by Lisa Harris
Kate Elliot trails her niece's kidnapper to Paris and teams up
with FBI agent Marcus O'Brian. Together, they must stay steps
ahead of the culprit, who is now after them as well.

PLAIN PERIL • by Alison Stone
Hannah Wittmer's Amish country homecoming is less than
welcome. Someone killed her nieces' mother...and Hannah
and her newfound protector Sheriff Spencer Maxwell are the
next targets.

SILENT HUNTER • by Maggie K. Black
Nicky Trailer is trapped on an island with a killer and the man
who broke her heart. Will Luke Wolf be able to save her life
and redeem her trust?

MANHUNT • by Lisa Phillips
When a fugitive escapes their custody, deputy US marshals
Eric Hanning and Hailey Shelder must battle floodwaters and
bullets in order to stay alive.

**LOOK FOR THESE AND OTHER LOVE INSPIRED BOOKS WHEREVER
BOOKS ARE SOLD, INCLUDING MOST BOOKSTORES, SUPERMARKETS,
DISCOUNT STORES AND DRUGSTORES.**

LISCNM0115

REQUEST YOUR FREE BOOKS!
2 FREE RIVETING INSPIRATIONAL NOVELS
PLUS 2 FREE MYSTERY GIFTS

YES! Please send me 2 FREE Love Inspired® Suspense novels and my 2 FREE mystery gifts (gifts are worth about $10). After receiving them, if I don't wish to receive any more books, I can return the shipping statement marked "cancel." If I don't cancel, I will receive 4 brand-new novels every month and be billed just $4.74 per book in the U.S. or $5.24 per book in Canada. That's a savings of at least 21% off the cover price. It's quite a bargain! Shipping and handling is just 50¢ per book in the U.S. and 75¢ per book in Canada.* I understand that accepting the 2 free books and gifts places me under no obligation to buy anything. I can always return a shipment and cancel at any time. Even if I never buy another book, the two free books and gifts are mine to keep forever.

123/323 IDN F5AC

Name	(PLEASE PRINT)	
Address		Apt. #
City	State/Prov.	Zip/Postal Code

Signature (if under 18, a parent or guardian must sign)

Mail to the Harlequin® Reader Service:
IN U.S.A.: P.O. Box 1867, Buffalo, NY 14240-1867
IN CANADA: P.O. Box 609, Fort Erie, Ontario L2A 5X3

**Are you a current subscriber to Love Inspired Suspense books
and want to receive the larger-print edition?
Call 1-800-873-8635 or visit www.ReaderService.com.**

* Terms and prices subject to change without notice. Prices do not include applicable taxes. Sales tax applicable in N.Y. Canadian residents will be charged applicable taxes. Offer not valid in Quebec. This offer is limited to one order per household. Not valid for current subscribers to Love Inspired Suspense books. All orders subject to credit approval. Credit or debit balances in a customer's account(s) may be offset by any other outstanding balance owed by or to the customer. Please allow 4 to 6 weeks for delivery. Offer available while quantities last.

Your Privacy—The Harlequin® Reader Service is committed to protecting your privacy. Our Privacy Policy is available online at www.ReaderService.com or upon request from the Harlequin Reader Service.
We make a portion of our mailing list available to reputable third parties that offer products we believe may interest you. If you prefer that we not exchange your name with third parties, or if you wish to clarify or modify your communication preferences, please visit us at www.ReaderService.com/consumerschoice or write to us at Harlequin Reader Service Preference Service, P.O. Box 9062, Buffalo, NY 14269. Include your complete name and address.

LIS13R

SPECIAL EXCERPT FROM

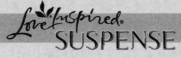

A woman's young son has gone missing.
Can he be found?

Read on for a preview of TO SAVE HER CHILD
by Margaret Daley, the next book in her
ALASKAN SEARCH AND RESCUE series.

"What's wrong, Ella?" Josiah's dark blue eyes filled with concern.

Words stuck in her throat. She fought the tears welling in her. "My son is missing," she finally squeaked out.

"Where? When?" he asked, suddenly all business.

"About an hour ago at Camp Yukon. I hope you can help look for him."

"Let's go. My truck is outside." Josiah fell into step next to her.

Ella slid a glance toward him, and the sight of Josiah, a former US marine, calmed her nerves. She knew how good he was with his dog at finding people. Robbie would be all right. She had to believe that. The alternative was unthinkable.

He opened the back door for his dog, Buddy, then quickly moved to the front door for Ella. "I'll find Robbie. I promise."

The confidence in his voice further eased her anxiety. Ella climbed into the cab with Josiah's hand on her elbow.

As he started the engine, Ella ran her hands up and down her arms. But the chill burrowed its way into the

Love Inspired

Love the Love Inspired book you just read?

Your opinion matters.

Review this book on your favorite book site, review site, blog or your own social media properties and share your opinion with other readers!

Be sure to connect with us at:
Harlequin.com/Newsletters
Twitter.com/LoveInspiredBks
Facebook.com/LoveInspiredBooks

HLIREVIEWSR

marrow of her bones, even though the temperature was sixty-five.

Josiah glanced at her. "David will get plenty of people to scour the whole park. Do you have anything with Robbie's scent on it?"

"I do. In my car."

He backed up to her black Jeep Wrangler. "Where?"

"Front seat. A jacket he didn't take with him."

Josiah jumped out of the truck to get it before Ella had a chance to even open her door.

He returned quickly with Robbie's brown jacket in his grasp.

He gave it to Ella. "This will help Buddy find your son."

Ella leaned forward, staring out the windshield at the sky. Dark clouds drifted over the sun. "Looks like we'll have a storm late this afternoon."

Josiah's strong jawline twitched. "We can still search in the rain, but let's hope that the weatherman is wrong."

Ella closed her eyes. She had to remain calm and in control. That was one of the things she'd always been able to do in the middle of a search and rescue, but this time it was her son.

"Ella, I promise you," Josiah said. "I won't leave the park until we find your son."

Will Robbie be found before nightfall?
Pick up TO SAVE HER CHILD to find out.
Available February 2015, wherever
Love Inspired® Suspense books and ebooks are sold.

Copyright © 2015 by Harlequin Books S.A.

LISEXP0115R